THE WHALE
SURFACES

THE WHALE SURFACES

PREQUEL
To
ESCAPING THE WHALE

Ruth Rotkowitz

ISBN Paperback: 978-1-7355756-2-9
ISBN Electronic: 978-1-7355756-1-2

Library of Congress Control Number: 2021904968

This is a work of fiction. Any references to historical events, real people, or real places are used fictitiously. Other names, characters, places and events are products of the author's imagination, and any resemblance to actual events or places or persons, living or dead, is entirely coincidental.

Printed in the United States of America.

Ruth Rotkowitz
www.RuthsWhale.com

PRAISE FOR
ESCAPING THE WHALE

"A Jewish story, a woman's story, a universal story about our struggle to defeat the demons – both human and imagined – that dare us to fight for our survival, our sanity, our humanity."
— Andrew Heinz, author of
Jews and the American Soul

"This fast-paced book examines topics of family, love, and self-preservation. A remarkable first novel."
— Sheryl Bronkesh, President,
Phoenix Holocaust Association

"It's hard to believe this riveting new novel about a young woman's struggle with her own inner demons is the author's debut."
— Michael Zam, author and co-creator of
Feud: Bette and Joan

"A beautifully written account of a young woman grappling with the emotional upheaval often associated with children of Holocaust survivors…You'll want to cheer Marcia on her journey!"
— Helen Locke, Education Committee,
Phoenix Holocaust Association

"A harrowing yet beautiful story I could not put down."
— Pamela Burke, PhD., social psychologist,
N.J. Council of the Arts Fellowship Recipient for Fiction

"Readers looking for a novel with psychological insight will enjoy ***Escaping the Whale***…A good read!
— Maxine Cooper, psychotherapist

INTRODUCTION

This novella is dedicated to the wonderful readers of my debut novel, *Escaping the Whale*.

Your involvement with my protagonist, Marcia Gold, touches me deeply. Your questions about Marcia's childhood and your requests to understand how she grew to be the 28-year-old woman in *Escaping the Whale* led to the creation of this prequel, *The Whale Surfaces*. I hope your questions are answered in this book.

Delving into a character's background is a fascinating exercise. Working backwards from the adult I originally created to identify the logical beginnings of Marcia's battle with her demons brought me face to face with the realization that most childhoods consist of a combination of light and darkness. Children of survivors face a unique situation, as darkness often forms a much larger component of their lives than is desirable. Each individual must discover his or her own way of overcoming these forces. As we see in *Escaping the Whale*, the struggle to lead a happy life in spite of the burden of inherited trauma is compounded by the shame and stigma attached to mental problems.

Inherited trauma, a form of Post Traumatic Stress Disorder (PTSD), has only recently been recognized as a real and serious phenomenon. Readers who have contacted me and people who have attended my talks have readily shared their own experiences with inherited trauma, as if floodgates have been opened. It is not only children of Holocaust survivors who may suffer from this affliction; people from diverse backgrounds suffer as well and relate to Marcia.

It is heartening to witness and participate in the increased openness among second and third generation survivors. The days of denial and suppression of our stories are ending. It is my hope that my two books about Marcia Gold can illuminate the darkness surrounding this topic, leading to healing and to empathy.

I am eternally grateful to you, my readers, for leading the way. May we all find the courage to identify and conquer our individual whales.

CHAPTER ONE

Eleven-year-old Marcia Gold was excited about her homework assignment. Sitting at the speckled Formica table beneath the fluorescent lights in the Brooklyn apartment kitchen, she spread out her notebook and pen.

"Good girl, doing homework," said her mother, coming into the kitchen and patting Marcia's head. Marcia waved her away, trying to concentrate.

The assignment: write a scene that occurs on a beach. Most of the class had either been to the beach over the weekend, when beaches had opened for the season, or were looking forward to going soon.

"Be creative!" the teacher, Mrs. Collings, had urged. They could start with something real, she explained, and then embellish it. Marcia liked that word "embellish." She thought it sounded musical. "And use lots of description!" were the teacher's final words on the assignment.

Marcia knew exactly what she was going to write. The warm glow she'd felt at the beach with her family had lasted through the rest of the day after her big brother Eliot, dripping wet as his trunks clung to his body, had emerged from the water. But that did not mean she'd forgotten the "vision" that had visited her there. It had stayed with her, vivid and sharp. That animal's slick gray sheen, the hugeness of its open mouth, the shock of the soldiers emerging. She could return to that any time. It was a personal possession, this vision, always waiting for her. And she was excited to write about it.

Marcia saw something no one else there had seen. Beneath one of the largest waves, the hump of a huge, gigantic animal momentarily appeared. She gasped. Was Eliot in danger? To her relief, she saw him coming out of the water then, taking her little sister Rochelle's hand to lead her back to their blanket. But that animal – she saw now that it was larger than she'd originally thought – was edging closer and closer to the shore. It emerged from the wave that had been its cover, and a humongous head lifted itself out of the water. Why aren't all the people scattering and screaming? Don't they see this? Aren't they scared?

The head, followed by a gargantuan, sleek gray body, opened its huge mouth, as if to vomit something onto the shore. And it did! Out of this immense mouth poured an army of soldiers. Marcia grabbed onto her father's leg. The soldiers were Gestapo – she could tell by the uniforms. Hundreds of them were marching, in goose-step just like she had seen in countless movies, just like her parents had described what they'd seen in their Polish towns, onto the beach. More and more were coming – how many were stored in that animal's mouth?! Marching in lock-step, they emerged from that open mouth, remaining in perfect formation as they approached.

"What's the matter?" her father asked, covering her hand with his own. Her nails were digging into the skin of his leg. "Are you okay?" She tried to tell him that the Nazi soldiers were heading straight for their blanket. They are probably looking at her parents and thinking: You got away from us once before – we are back for you now! Marcia had tried to tell her father this but the words stuck in her throat.

Marcia turned to her notebook and began her assignment with description. She described the smooth, dark blue water, the rolling waves, the foam, the laughing people. Then she went into the imagination part, and wrote what she saw as if it were really happening. It had seemed real to her at the time. She was very proud of her story when it was finished.

She came home crying from school the following day. "I hate Mrs. Collings!" she wailed and ran into her room.

Instead of appreciating the story's description and imagination, the teacher had been horrified by the story and had yelled at poor Marcia. "A beach is a place for beauty and peacefulness!" she had shouted in front of the class. "Why would you write this scary, crazy story! If you want a passing grade on it, you will write another one!"

The teacher had thrown the pages down on Marcia's desk and then went on to read aloud and praise MaryAnn's story, which involved throwing a ball back and forth on the sand with her sister. Marcia fought back tears and spent the rest of the day staring down at the papers on her desk. When the day was over, she gathered them up and ran out.

"What made you think of that?" her mother asked when Marcia tearfully reported the events of the day.

"I don't know," Marcia shrugged. "It just…came to me. I think I actually dreamed it one night, and then it came back that day at the beach. Kind of like a vision."

"She has bad dreams all the time," little four-year-old Rochelle piped up in her squeaky voice. Turning to Marcia, she added, "You scream in your sleep, and you wake me up!"

"I do not!" Marcia shouted.

"You do so!" Rochelle retorted. "I'm in the room with you! You scream your head off!"

"Enough, you girls," their father said. "First of all, dinner is getting cold, so stop arguing and eat. Secondly, Marcia, just write something else and be done with it." He spooned vegetables onto his plate.

"Why should I?" Marcia yelled. "You should go talk to her. Tell her she's an idiot! I was being creative, like she said! It just wasn't exactly the kind of creative she wanted. I'm not writing another one." She crossed her arms.

Her parents exchanged looks over her head. "Okay, don't," said her mother, sighing. "But take another piece of chicken."

"I just had a piece."

"It was a tiny drumstick. Not enough."

Marcia excused herself and stomped off to her room. Eliot wasn't there to stick up for her. He had basketball practice. Lucky Eliot.

The incident passed. Marcia never wrote another story, the teacher ignored it and did not penalize her, and Marcia spent the remaining few weeks of school shooting dirty looks at Mrs. Collings. Maybe the teacher forgot all about me and my "failing" composition, Marcia thought, because the assassination of President Kennedy months earlier dwarfed all the teacher's other concerns. Crying in class when the news was announced, Mrs. Collings seemed dazed the remainder of the year. The teacher's break from her mourning to yell at Marcia must have been her way of trying to act like a teacher after all. Of course, Marcia reasoned, if the death of the President had saved her from failing, that would be awful, a terrible burden of guilt to bear. She would have been willing to fail the grade if it would have kept President Kennedy alive.

She did have nightmares. Rochelle was right, and Marcia was mortified. She usually found excuses to avoid sleepovers because anyone else would make fun of her for screaming during the night. Everyone except her best friend Natalie, whose parents also came from some town in Poland, or maybe Ukraine. They weren't sure themselves. Marcia never knew if she screamed during the night when Natalie was there, but since Natalie sometimes talked and yelled in her sleep, Marcia knew it was all right. Neither her parents nor Natalie's ever seemed to hear the screams. In both apartments, the master bedroom was at the end of a long hallway, as far from the children's bedrooms as possible. Did whoever designed these Brooklyn apartments know that the children who would live here would scream at night and should be far from their parents? Maybe the screaming never lasted very long – perhaps it only seemed long to the person doing the screaming.

What happened in those nightmares? She couldn't always remember; she just knew they left her terrified and soaked in sweat. Scary things, mean people, sharp weapons aimed at her and her family, crowds chanting hateful slogans and goading people to do horrible things. Once, a laughing group of young men hanged a shop owner in front of his shop, and no one could do anything. They just stood around, wringing their hands and looking upset. She knew she had heard that story somewhere. It was all very vague, but horrifying nevertheless.

The following year in school, they studied Greek mythology. As soon as Marcia read about the Trojan Horse, she had half a mind to march back into Mrs. Collings's classroom and direct that misinformed excuse of a teacher to compare her story of soldiers pouring out of a sea creature's mouth with the myth of the Greek soldiers pouring out of the wooden horse. Maybe, Marcia wondered, something inside her mind was in tune with this ancient story.

She came to believe, later that year, at age 12, that something inside her was indeed primitive, barbaric. Her recurring vision of the giant sea creature planted that idea in her head, and the night the Beatles appeared on the Ed Sullivan Show reinforced that thought. She was alone in the apartment – thank goodness, she thought – and sat in a chair pulled up close to the television set. As they performed and screeched and shook their hair around their heads, Marcia screamed too. She couldn't help it. She wished she were there with the other screaming girls in the audience, the ones who were crying and covering their faces and itching to throw bras and slips onstage. Poor Ed Sullivan – she was certain he was not prepared for this. But something elemental inside her was no better than those girls at the performance. They were all animals inside.

CHAPTER TWO

"Why can't I?" she whined to Eliot one day, when she was a seventh grader. Eliot sometimes waited for her on the corner of her junior high school when he was going home from the high school several blocks away at around the same time. She never knew if he'd be standing there, but was always happy when he was. Proud of her tall, handsome, big brother, she loved walking with him.

"Just don't," he answered, looking both ways before gently placing his hand on her back to get them across the street.

"Almost everyone is having a parent come in. It's a festival of different cultures. They'll all talk about the countries their families came from, and bring food from those countries for us to taste, and play musi…"

"Do *not* ask Mom and Dad. They won't do it. It might…upset them."

Marcia pouted the rest of the way home. Everything was such a mystery. Her parents whispering at night in the kitchen when they thought the children were asleep, questions and conversations shut down with a look. Maybe when she reached Eliot's age, Marcia reasoned, she would understand.

"I mean it," he reminded her as they entered the apartment.

"Okay, okay, I won't." She slammed her bedroom door, wondering why everything was so mysterious, why they were so different, why nothing was ever explained. Rochelle was sitting on her bed, playing with a doll, and shot her a quizzical look and then calmly returned to the blonde, bikini-clad hunk of plastic in her lap.

The night in the Emergency Room is a night she knew she would always remember. What had alerted her parents? Her screaming? It must have gone on much longer than usual. And she simply could not stop. Maybe Rochelle became truly frightened and summoned them. They hovered over her as she writhed in her bed, their faces strained and confused, her father's striped pajama top buttoned all wrong. Why did she notice that?

They took turns rushing back to their room to get dressed, then waking Eliot to tell him he was in charge of Rochelle. Somehow, they got her downstairs and into their car. She was still screaming. It would not stop, much as she tried to suppress it.

"What is it? What are you screaming about?" her mother kept asking, as she sat with Marcia in the back seat. Her mother seemed annoyed, possibly angry. Years later, Marcia would realize her mother was most likely frightened. This was, after all, unheard-of behavior. Neighbors could hear. What would everyone think? And her mother did love her, so she was surely worried and scared as well.

Exasperated, her mother shook her head, muttering to herself as her father silently drove through the darkness. What was she saying? That this child has a wonderful life so what is she so upset about? Why can't she just talk to us and tell us why she is doing this? Marcia was certain that that was what her parents were thinking, whether they were saying it or not. Did they think she was choosing to do this?

Did her screaming stop when she got to the hospital? Marcia does not remember. She remembers being put in a wheelchair and wheeled into a small room and being questioned by a kindly, young doctor with a soft, gentle voice. She remembered his beard, full of blond hairs mixed in with brown. What kind of doctor was he? She did not know. She was finally able to speak but she had nothing to offer.

Why were you screaming and shaking so? A dream. Can you tell me about the dream? I don't remember it.

He nodded his head and studied her face. She looked away. His ears seemed too big for his head, she noticed. She was given an injection, and some pills to take at home for another two days.

For a week or so after this incident, Marcia felt her parents' eyes on her whenever they were home. Were they waiting for another eruption? She ignored their stares as best she could. Marcia felt their fear and confusion radiating toward her but could think of nothing to offer them as reassurance. She would just have to be "normal" – at least as normal as possible so they would not worry. They were too frightened to talk about it; she understood that as well. She would strive to be the kind of daughter who doesn't frighten her well-meaning parents. Could she be that? She would have to try.

"We don't have to mention to anyone else about the… you know…the visit to the hospital," her mother, squirming in her kitchen chair, said one Friday night at dinner. They would be visiting the grandparents the following day. Marcia shrugged. She got it. An unwritten rule in the family was to never upset the grandparents.

CHAPTER THREE

"How come Eliot doesn't have to come?" was all Marcia could think of as their car made its way through Brooklyn weekend traffic on Saturday.

"Eliot is in high school now. He has basketball and lots of homework," was the response from the front seat. Rochelle, beside her, was singing some lilting song to the curly-haired doll she'd brought along, and the song was getting on Marcia's nerves.

"It's not fair," Marcia complained.

Suddenly, her father yelled, "Not fair?! Not fair?! What's not fair? That you have grandparents who are alive when so many people have no grandparents! When so many grandparents were killed in Europe, like Mom's parents, never to see their children have children, never to see them have a better life, away from the monsters! You don't know how lucky you are!"

He had turned his head to yell at her, and spittle flew from his mouth. "Shhh, watch the road," her mother cautioned, placing her hand on her husband's arm. His face red and his mouth set in a stark line, he turned back, offering his daughters a view of his sweating, bald head and wrinkly neck. Marcia slumped down in her seat and remained silent the rest of the way.

In the middle of dinner one evening, the phone rang. Marcia's mother hurried into the hallway to answer it while her father gazed after her with a jittery look on his face.

No one in the family would call during the official family dinner hour, so it must be someone else.

Her mother returned and put her hand on her hip.

"Marcia," she said, "that was your Hebrew school teacher."

"Oh," said Marcia, looking down at her plate, where a dry-looking veal cutlet sat in the center, surrounded by a decoration of peas that Marcia had created."What did she say?"

"Don't give me that. You know what she said. That you had a temper tantrum in class today and you were disruptive."

Eliot let out a guffaw and then covered it with a cough. They ignored him.

"She said you slammed down your book and stalked out of the room. Her words."

"It was a creepy story!" Marcia yelled. "I was sick of the way she kept talking about it! And it was not a temper tantrum!"

"What story?" asked Rochelle, holding her fork aloft in the air, her small face barely visible above the top of the table.

"Jonah and the whale," mumbled Marcia. "Just wait. You'll get the pleasure of having to hear it one day too. A whale swallows Jonah and then spits him out!"

Marcia remembered the nausea that filled her throat and stomach and propelled her out of the classroom. The teacher was going on and on about how God was using the whale to let Jonah know that he couldn't get away from his duty. In the girls' bathroom, Marcia took deep breaths until the nausea passed. Her memory of that frightening vision she'd had at the beach on that Memorial Day weekend with her family felt uncomfortably close.

"A whale swallows him?" Rochelle repeated, her voice squeaky. Eliot smiled at his little sister and continued shoveling food into his mouth.

"Honey," Marcia's mother said, sitting down. "I don't see the story as creepy. I see it as hopeful." They all turned toward her.

"Hopeful?"

"Sure. Jonah is certain he will die when he gets thrown into the sea. But a whale saves him. He is safe and protected inside the whale. The ocean can't harm him."

"That's lovely, dear," said Marcia's father, patting his wife's hand.

"Why can't you see the bright side of things, honey?" Marcia's mother cajoled.

""The teacher made it sound like Jonah was being punished for trying to run away, for not doing what God ordered him to do. To her, the whale was a punishment."

"Well, sometimes you can look at a story your own way," said her mother.

"And not get in trouble besides," added her father.

"How could he live inside a whale with nothing to eat?" Rochelle piped up, her forehead puckered in thought. "How long was he in there?"

"Three days and three nights," announced Eliot. "See, I remember something from Hebrew school."

"Three!" yelled Rochelle gleefully. "Like the three little pigs!"

They all laughed at little Rochelle. "Maybe," Rochelle continued, relishing the attention, "the whale sent food down to him that the whale didn't chew up and eat!"

"Certainly a possibility," Marcia agreed. "Like a dumb-waiter!"

"There you go, dear," encouraged her mother. "Just try to look for the bright side."

High school, she discovered, was somewhat better. She met some new people and had a bit more freedom. She could go over to friends' houses without offering too many details, and if she came home late and hadn't called, she could usually get away with a story about a riveting home-work project they'd all been working on.

Sometimes, she just walked. Sometimes she ran. She would say she was going to so-and-so's house and just walk around the neighborhood, or take the bus to another neighborhood, and walk. Aimlessly. By herself. It felt like freedom. Alone, meandering along, noticing houses and trees and people and discarded trash in gutters. Sometimes people sitting out on stoops looked at her as she passed, or kids playing stoop ball ran around her, ignoring her. That was all okay, as long as no one bothered her. There were enough stories circulating at school about boys who hang out in front of their houses taunting girls who pass by – yelling out insulting comments about their looks, or blocking their way and laughing about it, even pulling on their clothing or their bags as they tried to pass. Marcia walked with purpose, quickly, and wondered if that's what protected her. Or maybe she'd just been lucky so far.

One day, on a whim, she stayed on the bus for a few more stops and discovered a park with a path for joggers. It was a beautiful, sunny day and she felt open to joining in. She waited until most of the joggers had passed and then got into the lane and began walking fast. It felt good and she began to run. Her legs aching a bit and wind blowing back her hair, she fell in love with running. Everything around her became a blur, and she was a moving rocket. She was not as fast as some of the runners who kept passing her, but that was fine. Running put her into a state of mind she could only think of as airy, where she had no purpose in life but to keep moving and feel the air. When she finished a run, she leaned over, hands on her knees, and breathed deeply. It felt as if she had truly accomplished something, and the world looked so much brighter, the colors of the flowers in the park more vivid, the playful squeals of the children in the nearby playground more joyful.

By the time she got home, she was no longer sweaty, so there was never a need to explain her running. That was good, because Marcia's mother had a 'thing' about running, as Eliot called it. She hated things that she said had no purpose. When she was hiding out in the forest in Poland during the war with a Jewish partisan group, she had to run for her life many times. That had a purpose. Running just to run? She spat out her contempt for that idea any time it came up.

CHAPTER FOUR

It was her first real girlfriend shopping expedition. A few of the girls she met at the high school newspaper staff meeting decided they should all go shopping together. Marcia's only shopping had been with her mother, when she was young. Lately, she had just picked up a few clothing items at stores near their home, on her own or with Natalie. But now, she had money from family birthday and Chanukah gifts, and this would be a girls' outing, with girls she liked. At least so far, she thought.

They met at an agreed-upon spot on the first floor of A&S. Marcia took the subway and entered the department store directly from the subway station. She was delighted that this option existed, as it had been raining when she left home. Marcia was practically skipping through the station. Giggling, the four girls greeted one another, complimenting this one's hair and that one's jacket, then took off for the women's and junior's clothing section.

Their arms loaded down with hangers trailing garments in all colors, the girls dashed into the fitting rooms, each taking one stall. "Whenever one of us is trying on something we might want, we'll come out here wearing it and call the rest of us out for our opinions," declared Denise, the only blonde among them who was aiming to be editor-in-chief of the school newspaper in her senior year.

Marie was the first to call the others out to the hallway of the fitting area. "What do you all think?" She twirled around in tight-fitting jeans and a somewhat transparent black top.

"You'd need to wear a black bra with that," said Jill, her arms folded across her chest as she judged.

"It's for a date," Marie explained. "Is it sexy?"

They all nodded their heads. "The pants are a little tight," Marie added, lifting up the top to show how her skin bulged slightly over the waist."

"Why don't you try the next size?" Marcia asked.

"It'll be too big. I want it to hug my body!" Marie declared, wiggling her tush. They all laughed.

"Okay, so this is a possibility," Marie conceded. "Back to our corners!" They all hustled back to their stalls, emerging whenever they had something to show the others.

It seemed to be going on forever. Marcia was sitting on the floor of her fitting room, staring into the mirror, looking at her pallid face, her brown hair clustering in messy waves, frizzy from the rain, her deadened expression. What had happened, she wondered. She'd been excited about this day, but now something had changed inside her. Then she looked over at the clothing she had hung up. Jeans, of course. And tops in blue and green and red and black. She turned away. It suddenly meant nothing. The clothes were hideous, garish. Her hands began to tremble. She wanted to run out of there, dump all those ridiculous clothes in the nearest trash can, scream into the rain.

"Come out, everyone!" called Denise. Her chirpy tone grated on Marcia's nerves, but she hoisted herself to her feet and joined the others. Denise was sporting a turquoise sweater with a low-cut neckline.

"Beautiful," Marcia said, hoping to rush the process along. The others all approved as well. Denise twirled around, checking herself in the mirror from various angles.

"Marcia, you haven't shown us anything," noted Jill after each of the others had paraded for the group in various outfits. "Didn't anything fit?"

Marcia shrugged. She had stopped trying on after one attempt. "Only one sweater, actually."

"Well, let's see it."

When Marcia emerged wearing the red turtleneck, the girls all approved. "Nice," they agreed.

"Personally, I hate turtlenecks," offered Denise. "They make me feel like I'm choking. But that's me."

At that moment, Marcia began to feel as if she were choking. She pulled the top of the sweater away from her neck.

"You have a good shape," said Jill. "Not too busty, like me," she added, looking down at her own chest, to the amusement of the others. "But not too flat. So you've got the build for a well-fitted sweater."

They all paid for their purchases, Marcia noticing that everyone else had bought more than one item. "Now we go for ice cream!" declared Marie, and they headed to a shop down the street. Marie decided they would each try a flavor she'd never tried before, and they all agreed. This resulted in many laughs when most of the ice cream ended up in the garbage. That included coconut marshmallow, peach-chocolate blast, pistachio peanut butter, and tutti frutti. At least the tutti frutti was colorful, with the multi-hued sprinkles across the top.

Sitting in the booth with the girls, tasting from one another's selections and laughing over the flavors, Marcia looked out the window at the steady drizzle and saw herself standing out there, looking in. Here was this happy group of friendly, nice girls – all good students – having a fun day together. Did she look like the others? Could this observer tell that she – this one girl in the group – was not enjoying herself, that she was apparently incapable of enjoying the ordinary pleasures of life that everyone else relishes? Why was she different? Why was she pretending to be present when she was actually suffering, aching to get away from them, to erase the entire shopping experience? What business did she have going off to A&S for this frivolous activity?

When she trudged into the apartment, her sneakers dragging on the floor, Marcia felt unsettled, a bit nauseous. She knew she should be feeling happy, contented. A nice day out with new friends, who all seemed to get along. A good time was had by all. So why was she feeling this way?

"So what did you get?" demanded Rochelle, who was sitting cross-legged on her bed.

"Oh, just a sweater."

"That's all? Why didn't you get anything else? You have enough money to get tons of new stuff. I spent all my money on sodas and comic books, but you could…"

"It doesn't matter," Marcia shot back. "I just wasn't in the mood."

Rochelle shook her head at her sister, and Marcia lay down on her bed, her face to the wall, to make Rochelle disappear.

That evening, there was a knock on her door. "Sweetheart, are you all right?" her mother called in. "You didn't want any dinner…"

"I'm fine."

"Are you sure?" Her mother opened the door a crack, peeking in. Marcia glimpsed the gray cardigan her mother wore in the house when the apartment was cold.

"Yes. I'm sure." She paused. "Actually, no."

Her mother stepped in, and Marcia felt the mattress shifting as her mother perched on the edge.

"What is it, honey?" she asked gently, rubbing Marcia's back with light strokes. Marcia bit her lip, but it was no use. She burst into tears.

"What's wrong with me, Mommy?" She hadn't called her mother Mommy in a long time.

"What do you mean?"

"I'm not like other people. I can't have fun. I can't enjoy anything. I'm sort of…crazy."

"You are not! You are a lovely, smart, beautiful, caring young lady!"

"Who can't go out with friends, like everyone else does, and just be normal!"

"Normal," said her mother, as if stating some unfortunate fact. "What's normal? Who decides?'

"I'm always somewhere else in my head! I'm always feeling guilty for having anything that other people can't have!"

"What other people?"

"Oh, other people! People in jail, people being tortured in third world countries, people starving and living on the streets…" Tears were pouring down her face and she began punching the wall near her bed.

Her mother gently pulled Marcia's fist away from the wall. "Honey, when I was your age…"

"I know, Mom. When you were my age, you were living in a forest, running for your life, scrounging for food, hiding from Nazis and Poles! That's part of it! You couldn't have this!"

"That's what I'm trying to explain. The life we were living, in the forest, was normal then. What were our options? Lie down and wait to die? Go back to our village and get killed? We accepted our normal at the time, expecting it to change one day. I would have been thrilled to have this kind of life that you have, these chances for simple joys. I dreamed of having it."

"But you never could. You never got to be a teenager."

"Not really."

"So why should I, or anyone, get that chance, if you couldn't have it?"

"Because I want you to have it! I couldn't have it but I can give it to you, my daughter! Why do you think I've told you kids about my years during the war?"

"Because it happened, it's the truth. And it's a big part of your life."

Her mother shrugged. "For one thing, even though it was hard, I always felt luckier than the people who were massacred, or taken away. We didn't know about the concentration camps yet but we knew being taken away was not good. And I've told you because I want you to see how much luckier you are, so you can appreciate what you have!"

"But it just makes me feel that I don't deserve it! Like I'm a worthless parasite!"

Her mother sat back as if she'd been slapped.

"What's going on in here?" Her father, scowling, poked his head into the doorway, thus stamping an end to the conversation.

"Nothing. Marcia and I are just talking," her mother said in a near-whisper, then got up and joined her waiting father. She looks sad, defeated, Marcia observed, watching her mother's back, slightly stooped, move away.

CHAPTER FIVE

··

The following day, the news blazed with the end of what was to be known as the Six-Day War. Israel had been attacked by the Arabs, once again, and had won, once again, this time capturing the Old City of Jerusalem as well as the West Bank, the Sinai, and the Golan Heights. The world was agog with this military success, and all the Jewish tenants in her building were walking around with big grins on their faces and their heads held high, smiling broadly at one another instead of simply rushing past. The bright sunshine of the June day seemed to be shining on all Jews. Her mother talked on the phone with one of her cousins in Israel. Their children, all in the army, were alive and unharmed. Everyone was celebrating. Marcia was most moved by a photograph of a slight, dark-skinned Israeli soldier spontaneously hugging the sturdy Prime Minister Golda Meir at the Wall. There were tears in everyone's eyes. What a victory. The image of the meek ghetto Jew who could be easily slaughtered was being shattered.

I should move to Israel, Marcia thought. Help fight for the country. Do something good, something useful, not waste my life here with nonsense. I would have a purpose then. She would re-visit that idea in the future, she knew.

She cut out of a magazine a photograph of a few Israeli soldiers, soldiers who had recaptured Jerusalem, viewed from the back, praying at the Wall with a large tallit – a prayer shawl – spread around all their shoulders. Soldiers who were completely secular, not religious at all, felt moved to wrap themselves in a prayer shawl, put yarmulkes on their heads, and pray. It brought tears to her eyes. She kept it on her night stand. There was joy in the future, she knew it then. And when President Johnson appointed Thurgood Marshall to the Supreme Court that same month, making him the first Black person on the high court, this added to her optimism. Change for the better was possible!

Still filled with optimism as the new school term got underway, Marcia accompanied her girlfriend group from the newspaper to the movies one late December day to see *The Graduate*, and she was actually able to enjoy the experience, getting engrossed in the story on the screen. All the girls loved it. Maybe she was learning to be normal after all, she thought. When she returned home, she listened to her Simon & Garfunkel album over and over again on the little record player in her room, replaying the songs that were used in the movie. Lying on her bed, listening to the music, she felt that everything could be good.

For the following two summers, Marcia worked as a counselor at a day camp, corralling a group of six-and seven-year-olds to various activities, being as sweet as possible to parents when they dropped off and picked up their kids. In July of her second year as a counselor, when Apollo 11 landed on the moon and Neil Armstrong's "one small step for man, one giant leap for mankind" line became a famous mantra, she warmed to the excitement of the kids over that event. They were part of history in the making, and they knew it.

She had them draw pictures of the moon and an astronaut stepping on it. The pictures were heartwarming, some hilarious. The astronaut was depicted by most of them as a robot with a big smile visible on his face through his helmet. They loved the fact that he'd planted an American flag, and the flag made it into lots of their pictures. A few kids, unwilling to abandon the image of the moon perpetuated in their children's books, just drew a romantic-looking crescent moon shining in a dark sky. One child even painted a smile on the moon's face. That's fine, Marcia thought, complimenting all of them on their work, patting their little heads as she made the rounds. Reality will hit those kids one day, she thought, whether about the moon or about everything else in life.

Later that summer, when Woodstock dominated the news and the parents Marcia encountered every day were busy tut-tutting about it as they leaned on their car hoods in their shorts chatting while waiting for their children, Marcia knew not to bring that up with six-and seven-year-olds. A music festival was one thing to explain, but some of the kids watched the news with their parents at night and she was not prepared to answer questions about drugs or sex. Would she ever be? Probably not. Would she ever attend an event like that? An event that could get out of control? She knew the answer to that.

Unfortunately, her euphoria did not last. About a month before her high school graduation, the country was stunned by the Kent State deaths. Students protesting the Vietnam War were shot at by National Guard troops called in. Everyone lamented the tragedy. At school, all the kids shook their heads mournfully, their eyes big with fear. One of the students killed, it was reported, was just there to see what it was all about. Be careful where you go and who or what you associate with – that seemed to be the message from adults to children.

"Terrible, terrible," murmured her mother that evening in front of the news report. "Those kids should be studying, not out there looking for trouble. That's what they're in college for, right?"

"They weren't doing anything illegal. They were protesting the war," Marcia said wearily. "Peaceful protest is their right. You can disagree with the government here, you know."

"So they say," her mother mumbled. "It's always a possible danger, though. No matter what. The government knows who you are once you go to one of those things," she added, waving her hand at the TV screen.

The news continued its report, indicating that those National Guardsmen had no experience with situations like that and might have simply panicked. The parents of one of the students who'd been gunned down tearfully answered questions from their living room couch, clutching each other's hands and showing a framed photo of their son at his high school graduation. A big smile lit up his face. He had hopes and dreams and plans, they pointed out. Now, Marcia realized, he will always be the boy in that picture to those parents, locked in that age, stuck in the amber-glue of time, like a fossil.

Why is the world full of so much pain, Marcia wondered, closing her eyes. Does it ever end? And will danger always lurk in the unlikeliest places, ready to pounce on the unsuspecting? Marcia found herself shivering whenever she pondered those kids mowed down at Kent State. What more could happen in the world?

CHAPTER SIX

Marcia thought of her growing-up years as a prelude. A prelude to what – real life? Personal contentment? Joy and abandon? No more nightmares? In the years that passed, she thought of herself as keeping her head down and getting through it all, until college. When she was about to graduate high school, Marcia couldn't wait for college. College will be the answer – she just knew it. Everything will be different; she'll be different. Better. Even though she would be living at home and attending the closest city university, Brooklyn College, she was convinced it would be the beginning of a new life. She saw how Eliot's years in college rendered him pretty much immune to household rules and family expectations. He was gone from the apartment a lot of the time, and it wasn't always for classes. The best part, to Marcia, was that the most vague and cursory explanations he provided for his whereabouts were not questioned. Marcia couldn't wait.

Wading through crowds of students protesting the Vietnam War just to get to her classes was unnerving. She understood their outrage, but when she got shoved or elbowed or when someone screamed into her face, her identification with the protesters was sorely tested. Crowds terrified her; she couldn't say why. What if she got trampled in a riot? What if police came with their batons and dogs and guns, as they'd done years earlier at the Birmingham march, and indiscriminately attacked? They wouldn't ask if she was just passing through, trying to get to a class. They would not stop to look at her and realize that she is a good, conscientious student with no interest in causing trouble. What if the protesters began to turn on one another, each accusing others of not being zealous enough in their beliefs or their efforts? People in a mob were different than they were on their own and could not be trusted.

The first class Marcia attended, after skirting a demonstration on the lawn outside that was just getting underway, was filling with students when she arrived. She didn't recognize anyone from her high school there, a fact she liked. She immediately slid into a seat in the back row, near the back door. Most of the rooms seemed to have a door near the front and another near the back. Perfect. Why? She knew why. So she could feel safe. She could watch everyone else but no one could stare at her without her knowing. With alphabetical seating plans, which most of the high school teachers used, she always ended up in the middle of the room, feeling that all eyes were on her and that everyone could tell when she felt uncomfortable or embarrassed. She was on a stage, being judged. Now, she could sit back in her last row seat and see everyone else. It was wonderful, feeling superior.

Besides, who knows what could happen? Stormtroopers in big boots, Nazis with rifles, anyone at all could suddenly burst into the room and start killing, or hold them all hostage, or pick one or two people to torture in front of the others. But she, in her chosen seat, would be able to make a quick getaway out that back door, if need be.

"We're all here because our parents couldn't bear to let us go out-of-town," grumbled a bleached-blonde girl who was sitting in front of her. As they all waited for the professor to arrive, Marcia took out a notebook and pen and put them on the desk.

"They don't want to lose control over us," added another.

"Maybe they can't afford it," Marcia offered, thinking of her own family's squeezed finances.

"That's bullshit," came a voice from the other end of the room. "So many scholarships are available. You just have to know how to apply for them."

"That means you have to have gone to a high school with a guidance counselor who knows how to help you with that," offered a male voice from somewhere. Chortles and chuckles followed.

"Knowing how isn't the issue. It's being willing to bother. You know, it takes time away from filing your nails, or reading a magazine at your desk."

"My guidance counselor said: 'Oh just go to Brooklyn College' when I came in one day with a bunch of brochures about a scholarship at a school I liked."

Marcia nodded at the voice imitation this student had perfected, the snarky put-down. "She didn't even look up at me when she said it."

They all quieted down when the professor, looking quite professorial in a nubby brown cardigan and graying beard, entered the room. But the conversation stayed in Marcia's head. Was it true, that it was not impossible to go to an out-of-town college? Of course, tuition was only part of the expense – there were so many other expenses involved. Her family could never have afforded it. Of course, they never would have agreed to it either. Like one of her classmates had said, they were not ready to give up control, or they were too afraid of the big bad world out there. Marcia sometimes thought that her family believed they could live in the United States and send their children to public schools but still hold on to the small-village, shtetl way of life they'd experienced. Is it possible to have it both ways?

Marcia acknowledged the griping of the others but was willing to dismiss it, as she was determined to make college matter. She would use it to expand her mind and her social life. She would not permit negativity to mar her experience. Whether or not she had to be in Brooklyn College, she vowed to use the four precious years to grow up, expand her horizons, blossom, flourish, plan a future for herself, become independent, LIVE. Eliot had graduated college half a year early, and had taken off for a job in Atlanta. The fact that his lottery number for the Vietnam War draft was a good one allowed him to do that. If he could do it, so could she. Marcia knew he was having the time of his life – rooming with two other guys, working at some lab, planning to eventually go to graduate school for chemistry, meeting lots of other young people, dating. He came home for weekends on rare occasion, and her parents fussed over him.

"Eat this, it's your favorite soup," her mother would coax, and Eliot would laugh. "I bet you don't get good food like this in Georgia." Her mother tried to imitate a Southern accent but it fell flat, and Eliot laughed again.

"When are you going over to see your grandparents?" her father would ask. "They haven't seen you in so long!" Eliot laughed again. "I was here a few weeks ago, it's not so long," he protested. Seeing his father's expression, he added, "Sure. I'll go over later today."

Did her parents notice that her brother was coming home less and less frequently? Did they realize they were scaring him away instead of luring him back? Or maybe an independent life was so wonderful he had no desire to come back too often.

"So how's it going, sis?" Eliot asked on one of his visits home in early summer, when they were alone on a drive, heading to the beach. She shrugged. Things were actually not as exciting as she had hoped they would be. He seemed to read her mind.

"Don't worry, everything takes time," he said.

Suddenly, the tears came pouring out. "Hey, hey, what's going on?" Eliot said. He pulled off the road.

Marcia wanted to punch herself. She'd been so looking forward to this time with her big brother, and now this onslaught of tears was going to ruin everything. She and Eliot were heading to the beach, which Eliot said he missed. Rochelle was at a friend's house and Marcia was thrilled that she would have her brother to herself.

"Oh, just everything," she whispered, grabbing the tissue Eliot was handing her. "Just…I don't know." She cried some more. Eliot just waited, sitting quietly.

"College isn't a magic bullet, you know." He paused. "Nothing is, actually."

"So there's no chance for anything to change?"

"Not true. You just have to make the effort. You know, be open. Open to meeting new people. Meeting…guys."

She almost told him that guys didn't seem interested in her, but she held that back. "I'm in a house plan. We have parties. I go to them." Her voice was a monotone.

"And…?"

"I'm not a party person. Hate crowds. Everyone looking you up and down, sizing you up. I just want to get out of there. Wherever I am, it seems, I want to get away. If I'm inside, I want to be outside. If I'm outside, I want to be on another street somewhere. I hate feeling invisible and ignored, and I also hate being noticed and judged. There's no answer for me. I never want to be at a party, that's for sure. "

"Forget parties for now. They're not for everyone. Just be relaxed and open, doing your regular casual stuff. But look around you while doing them, be aware, you know, open to possibilities."

Marcia wiped her face. "Let's go."

She stood at the shoreline, watching Eliot. The water lapping at her feet felt good. She inched in a bit farther. Eliot is such a good swimmer, she thought, watching as he dove beneath one wave at a time, rising just to tackle the next wave. He was so muscular and agile – he probably had tons of girlfriends. She recalled that long-ago beach trip on Memorial Day when she'd had that frightening vision of a giant creature emerging from the waves, and then tried to write about it for some moronic teacher. She shook her head, dismayed by the memory of that experience.

A little boy nearby was digging in the sand, filling a little green plastic pail. Suddenly, a wave washed up onto the shoreline, hitting Marcia above the knees and knocking over the little boy's pail. Marcia watched as the little boy calmly emptied his pail and moved back onto dry sand. He didn't cry or get upset, she noted, impressed. She also backed up a bit. That's the problem with the ocean, she thought. One minute the water ends in one spot, and the next minute, it moves onto the sand and ends in a new spot. Totally unpredictable. Who's to say it won't at some time overwhelm the entire beach, possibly keep moving into the town?

When Eliot was getting ready to go back to Atlanta, their mother bustled about the kitchen, packing sandwiches and cookies for him. "Mom," he groaned. "It's not that long a flight. Believe me, I won't starve."

"You never know," she countered, reaching for the Saran Wrap. "The plane could be delayed, or it might have to circle for hours before landing. Or you might get home and be hungry and find nothing in the fridge. Maybe your roommates ate everything while you were gone."

Eliot and Marcia exchanged a look. He headed back to his room to finish packing just as Rochelle walked in, smelling of cigarettes. "Hey, what's going on?" she asked.

"Your brother is leaving today," snapped their mother. "Where were you?"

Rochelle shrugged. "At Janet's. I told you."

"Say goodbye to him. You hardly saw him while he was here." Their mother glared at Rochelle.

"Brush your teeth," Marcia whispered, and Rochelle nodded. Marcia found her sister an amazing enigma. Brilliant in math but a regular social butterfly, constantly attending one party or another, Rochelle seemed to nurture both parts of herself without any trouble.

"How do you switch off one half of yourself to jump into the other?" she once asked Rochelle as she watched her slam her math book shut and begin applying makeup for a supposed visit to a friend, which meant a party or a meet-up with a secret boyfriend. Rochelle had shrugged. "It's no big deal," she'd replied. "Everyone is more than just one thing." Marcia stared as her sister applied black eyeliner with a steady hand. The line was straight and close to the lashes, as liner should be. Maybe that's applied math, Marcia had thought grudgingly.

Rochelle had a much more active social life in middle school than Marcia ever had. As Marcia watched her sister get ready for an outing, she thought Rochelle's easy success must lie in her hair, which was long and straight as a pin, as opposed to Marcia's, which was wavy, curly, unruly, frizzy at times, and impossible to grow long. Rochelle could easily comb her hair straight down, sideways over one eye, pulled back in a clip or ponytail, or wrapped up in an elaborate bun. Straight hair did what you wanted it to do, and Rochelle could switch personas as smoothly as she could switch hairstyles. Marcia wondered if that was the reason – or part of the reason, at least – that Rochelle could manage her two lives, social and academic, so successfully. Staring more intently at her sister, Marcia had to chuckle, as she was certain she detected a few well-placed blonde streaks in Rochelle's hair. She had to hand it to Rochelle, managing that and evading the scrutiny of the family dinner table/ interrogation room.

Eliot too, like Rochelle, managed his life well, enjoying himself and his freedom while remaining in the good graces of their parents. Was she the only child in the family floundering? She would work on that. That week, Marcia kept Eliot's words close; in fact, she felt them floating in her chest. Wherever she went, she looked around, checking out other students. Some smiled at her, some did not. She tried to be "open," as he had advised, and she thought she knew what he meant. She felt herself opening not only her eyes, but her heart and her soul. Open. That became her mantra. She took deep breaths and imagined herself opening to the world, like a flower blooming in the sun, its petals branching out to the world. It felt…hopeful. Hopeful and warm. She even found herself laughing whenever a professor took attendance by reading out names from a list and the students answered "Present." She imagined a classroom with only one student sitting there and answering "Present" to every name and the professor, who never looked up from the list, did not notice that only one student was sitting in the room. Chuckling at this imagined scenario one day in a math class, she noticed a few of the other students smiling at her. She felt a part of something then.

Heading to the subway to go home one day, she passed the luncheonette that was generally full of Brooklyn College students. Since it was summer session, there were not as many students around. She had gone into that luncheonette a few times with Natalie, and once with a group from her English class. She could go in by herself, she realized. Why not? Be open. Open.

She stood in line to order. She felt like squirming, like adjusting her backpack and scratching an itch on her scalp, but she managed to maintain a normal demeanor. She looked around but did not see anyone she recognized. That's okay, she told herself. I'm okay. She heard laughter from the back of the line and turned to look. A few guys were together, joking around.

That group of guys ended up seated at a table near hers, where she was sipping a coffee and nibbling at an English muffin. "You need this chair?" one of the guys asked. When she shook her head no, he took it for their table. Glad I served a purpose, she muttered to herself.

"Do I know you?" a voice behind her asked. She was back out on the sidewalk, slinging her pocketbook over her shoulder. She turned to see one of the guys who'd followed her outside. He smiled. His teeth were crooked and stained, which she found endearing. He was scruffy, with overgrown blondish hair and the beginning of a beard, and he was tall and skinny, wearing worn jeans and a wrinkled t-shirt of indeterminate color. He looked like someone she would like to cuddle up with.

Eliot's voice echoed in her head. Be open. "I don't think so." She made herself smile.

"I think you're in one of my classes. Geology?"

"Uh, maybe." Geology was the only class she had that was held in a big lecture hall, with the requisite assigned seats she so dreaded. Maybe he did notice her there. And maybe that wasn't bad at all.

He came closer. "I'm Gus," he said. "Hi."

"Marcia," she replied. They walked to the subway together, chatting. He was easy to talk to, she found. He was…open. Yes, that was the word for it all right. Before she knew it, he had taken her phone number and address. They would be going out over the weekend.

He was coming to the apartment to pick her up. How was that going to go? In high school, the kids – male and female – generally met in a group at the bowling alley or the local diner. Once in a while, a group came up to the apartment, and her parents barely seemed to notice. Somehow, she knew this would be different.

She paced the hallway, waiting for the doorbell to ring. "Yoo hoo!"came a familiar voice through the wall. Her mother hurried to the little doorway in the wall and unlocked it. The door opened to a vast, black space. It was the dumbwaiter, meant for sending garbage down to the super but used by Marcia's mother and her aunt upstairs as a direct phone line.

"Yes, dear! How are you?" her mother shouted, sticking her head into the opening and craning her head upwards toward her aunt's voice.

Great, Marcia muttered to herself. The sight of her mother's back and rear end protruding out of that hole in the wall always upset her. It seemed so dangerous. What if the super or one of the tenants suddenly decided to send up the container for the garbage and the two women were too immersed in their conversation to notice? They would be decapitated. Or if her mother ever leaned in too far, she could…Marcia couldn't even think of it. Why did her aunt have to initiate one of these conversations just now, when Marcia was waiting for her date, pacing like a caged animal?

"You must really like this guy," commented Rochelle. "Is he hot?"

"Go away!" Marcia shot back. Rochelle laughed on her way to their bedroom. Her father was just coming into the living room as Marcia sensed someone outside the door. She opened it to find Gus with his hand in the air, about to knock. Could she avoid introducing him?

"Hello there," said her father from behind her, putting out his hand. They shook. "This is Gus," Marcia said. "Bye!"

Gus laughed appreciatively as they headed down the stairs. "I like the way you handled that," he said. Marcia chuckled, thinking that she'd saved him from an uncomfortable encounter, one that might make him want to run away and never return.

"The building we live in is just like this," he added as they approached the stairway. "No elevator."

"Does it also have a dumbwaiter?"

"Sure."

"I hate that thing."

He took her hand when they reached the street. His hand was warm and comforting. "I guess it's better than carrying garbage down to cans in the alley."

Marcia found herself agreeing with that, as an alley could be dangerous, especially at night.

By the time the movie was over, Marcia couldn't remember a thing about it. They had whispered to each other the entire time. She felt she knew his life and understood his family and his easygoing ways. Why couldn't she be easygoing? It was such an amazing way to be.

She was curious about his name. Gus. "It's really Augustus," he'd explained, crinkling his nose. "Not a name I wish to go by. My dad was into Roman history when I was born, apparently. And they wanted – or had to – name me after his father, Abraham. So they used the "A.""

Abraham, huh? Marcia thought, smiling in the dark theater. It might please her parents to hear that, she thought.

He had a friend with an apartment near the college, he told her after the movie, and they were invited over. Marcia, for some reason, felt energized to hear that. She felt safe with Gus. If she were to feel anxious or uncomfortable at this friend's place, she believed she could tell him and they would leave.

As it turned out, the evening was fine. The friend was totally stoned when they got there, and two other couples arrived shortly after they did. This friend had dropped out of college and had some kind of job – in construction, she thought Gus had said – and his apartment had become a kind of communal hangout for his friends. A guitar was produced. The friend played, and so did Gus. He had a good singing voice too. They sang Dylan songs as well as Joan Baez, Judy Collins, Pete Seeger, Peter, Paul and Mary. "Blowin' In The Wind" seemed to be the group favorite, and Marcia joined in the chorus.

It was a jolly night. Beer appeared, with pretzels and stale chips. Marcia wondered about one of the other girls, who had hugged Gus when she arrived and playfully plopped down on his lap during a break from guitar-strumming. Marcia knew she could never behave that way with the other guys there, even if they became friends. And maybe Gus and this gal were more than friends, or had been once? She decided she would not let any such concerns get in the way of her 'new life.' They kissed when

Gus took her home. He kissed her hard and held her body close for a while. Marcia was tingling as she placed her hand on his chest. They would get together next weekend as well. She skipped to her room afterwards. Her life, perhaps, was beginning.

She and Gus became a couple. Marcia was filled with lightness. There was never any doubt that they would sleep together. She was ready. She would be moving into the next phase of her life. The sex with Gus was a wake-up call. He clearly found her attractive and wanted her, and that in itself was a turn-on. She was certain she was in love.

"His Hebrew name is Avraham," she informed her parents when they made a comment about his messy, long hair, which Marcia loved to run her fingers through when they lay together in his friend's bed. The friend had given Gus the key to his apartment.

"So he's Jewish," her mother said. "He could still get a haircut."

"Oh, please," Marcia responded, rolling her eyes as she left the kitchen.

"At *least* he's Jewish," she heard her father say after she had exited the room.

"See you later!" she yelled, pulling on her jacket.

"Where are you going? It's almost dinnertime!"

As she got to the door, her father intercepted her. "Your mother just asked you a question. You don't ignore her and just walk out. Answer!"

Her father had that expression Marcia recognized. She knew he meant business. "I'm going to the college library. I'm doing research for a paper." She reached for the door handle but her father held it shut. "Now? It's almost dark and we are eating dinner soon!"

Marcia felt a hot ball of something rise from her chest into her throat. "I am in college now! If I were at an out-of-town school, you wouldn't know when I was going out!

When Eliot was in college, he didn't have to answer for his every move!"

"That's different!" her father yelled back at her.

"Why is it different?"

"Because Eliot's a boy, dummy," Rochelle chimed in on her way to the kitchen.

"Stay out of this, Rochelle," said her father without taking his eyes off Marcia. "You are not going anywhere now. It's too late."

"That's not fair!" Marcia screamed.

"Not fair?! Not fair, did you say?!" yelled her father into her face, his face turning purple. "What do you know about what's not fair! I'll tell you what's not fair! Having no real childhood or adolescence, seeing your family and your neighbors murdered before your eyes, being marched into a ghetto to starve and live 14 to a dingy room, being marched to a concentration camp, being woken up at three in the morning in the freezing winter and forced to stand outside barefoot for hours, seeing others dropping dead in the snow! That's what's not fair! So don't you dare give me 'not fair,' young lady! Get into the kitchen and have dinner with the rest of the family!"

Marcia's tears poured from her eyes and she set her mouth. Of course, her father was right. Who was she to complain – compared to her parents' lives, she had it easy. How dare she resent anything about them, about her life? Maybe she *was* a worthless, spoiled parasite. She stalked into the kitchen, her jacket still on, sat in her seat, and when her mother placed a plate in front of her bearing an overcooked lamb chop and some dry-looking mashed potatoes, she wolfed it all down, tasting nothing. Nothing but tears waiting inside her throat.

"There! I ate! Do I have permission to go now?" She knew she was supposed to apologize to her father, but she simply could not do that.

"Watch that attitude!" Her father was clearly in one of his moods, Marcia noted. "So you're going to the library, huh?" he said. "Any chance your hippie guy will be meeting you there?"

"He has a name."

"I asked if you'll be meeting him." Her father was glaring at her from across the table. Am I some kind of evil, scheming, loose woman? she wondered. I have a boyfriend. He's nice and likes me. What's wrong with that? She was about to declare that Eliot had not had to answer questions like these, and that this was like a police interrogation.

She took a deep breath instead. "He is free to go to the library any time he wants," she said, her voice calm. "But no, we have no plans to meet."

"You see him enough."

"What's your problem with him anyway?"

"He's got no ambition. He's wishy-washy."

Marcia burst out laughing. Her father had once asked him what his major was and he'd shrugged and said he hadn't decided yet. When asked what kind of work he was interested in, he'd shrugged again. Marcia found his shrugging and his lopsided grin totally adorable. She just wanted to crawl into his lap and bury her head in his shaggy chest when he shrugged like that. It was true that he had no clear-cut ambition, no easy-to-define life plan. That was part of his allure, she knew.

"Okay, he's wishy-washy. Can I go now?"

CHAPTER SEVEN

The following day, after math class, she and Natalie had a heart-to-heart about Gus and Natalie's boyfriend of the moment, Jamie – specifically about their parents' disapproval. "Yeah, I just tune them out when they say stuff like that," Natalie said, chewing on a French fry. "If I'd let them get me upset every time, I'd be in a loony bin."

"I feel like I'm in a loony bin right now," grumbled Marcia. "I can't wait to be on my own! How do you tune them out? I wish I could."

"It takes practice," Natalie advised, dragging her next French fry through a puddle of ketchup. "But at first, it takes concentration. You focus, and then work on it."

"That simple, huh?" Her own French fries were cold and she pushed them away.

"It's not simple. But it's important. It's a survival skill, dearie. Trust me." Her own fries finished, she pulled Marcia's toward her, flipping her long, straight brown hair behind her back.

"Does Jamie ever talk about…the future?"

"You mean, like a future for us?"

"Just…the future."

Natalie thought for a moment. "Not really. I mean, he says he wants to work on Wall Street. He's majoring in Economics. That's the only thing he mentions occasionally. And I don't give a shit. We're not going to stay together, I know that. For now, it's fine."

"Gus talks about quitting school and heading out West. To California."

"Ah, the golden frontier. Actually, I can see him hitch-hiking cross country, his guitar slung across his back, his long hair blowing in the wind. He's a free spirit all right."

After a pause, Natalie pushed her dark bangs out of her eyes and studied Marcia. "Does that kind of talk bother you?"

"I don't really believe it, to tell you the truth. I think it's all talk. He might start a band, he says, or take odd jobs there, hang out on the beach, bla bla."

"You and I – we've never known anyone who actually did that. So it's hard to believe someone we know really would," Natalie mused, munching on a fry. "But there are people who do drop out. Would you be hurt if he did take off?"

It was Marcia's turn to pause. "You know, this will sound weird, because we do spend a lot of time together, and I love being with him, as you know."

Natalie chuckled. "Yes, you do exude that radiant, just-got-laid glow on a regular basis now."

Marcia shot her a sideways look. "As I was saying, I think I'd be okay with it. We've had a good run. I would understand."

"Don't be too understanding. The world is full of people – mainly guys – all too ready to take advantage of that."

"Gus isn't like that." Natalie nodded in agreement. "I'm happy for what we have. I'll always be happy for it. But he's not a student. Maybe dropping out of school and finding another path is what he should do."

"I can just see your folks' reaction to that."

"Can we leave them out of this? I'd like to believe that being 19 and a college student means I'm not a little kid any more. That I have my own life, and I'm entitled to some fun."

"Fun. Now that's a concept neither of our parents can grasp." Natalie shoved the last French fry into her mouth.

Marcia sipped her soda and felt guilt wash over her. Of course their parents didn't know from fun. The years that should have been fun were stolen from them. It was all about survival. Even after the war, after they got to the United States, they had to adjust to a new country, learn a new language, try to find out who had survived and who had not, and find a way to make a living. She had grown up on the stories of their difficulties in America. Both of them clearly possessed determination and resilience, which Marcia did admire. But fun? Hah! Did *she* have a right to want it? Maybe it's a genetic impossibility, if there is such a thing.

"What do you see in that guy?" her father demanded one evening after dinner, when Gus had come home with her and eaten with the family. He'd winked at her as he left the apartment, filling Marcia's stomach with happy flutters.

"Would you rather I be with no one?" she shouted. He makes me feel alive, wanted, she yearned to scream, thinking of his warm hands on her body, the sense of being part of something, of someone, when he entered her.

"There are other young men, more suitable…"

"I'll tell you what I see in him," she shouted back. "He's easy! He's easy to be with!"

"Easy? What's so great about easy?" Her father pushed his tea cup away and sat back, staring at her with beady, glistening eyes.

"Easy is relaxing! He's like a burst of sunshine!"

"Sunshine?" Her father looked confused. Marcia suddenly had the thought that to Gus, she could probably be any girl, that he would be with anyone. Instead of feeling hurt by that thought, it made her laugh. But seeing her father's expression brought back her anger.

"Being with him, after being here, is a relief!"

"A relief?"

Everything here is so…hard, so…intense! I'm sick of it!"

"You're sick of it?"

Are you just going to repeat everything I say?" Marcia shot up, nearly toppling her chair.

"Watch how you talk to your father!" her mother admonished from the sink, where she was washing dishes.

"Why don't you help your mother," her father grumbled, looking off to the side.

Why don't *you*, she felt like saying. But she dutifully joined her mother at the sink, drying dishes with such a vengeance she expected them to crack in half. All the while, standing at the sink, she visualized racing outside into the chilly air and opening her mouth wide to let out a scream – a scream so roaring and endless that the tightness and rage inside her would simply explode, bursting into the darkness like a volcanic eruption, a tsunami of everything that had ever been stomped upon bursting forth into the empty atmosphere. It was incredible to her that this did not show and she simply appeared, to any onlooker, like a regular teenage girl helping her mother with dishes.

After that evening, Marcia avoided speaking to her parents as much as possible. When her mother stuck her head into the dumbwaiter opening, she retreated to her room, furious. Why couldn't her mother recognize the danger in that contraption? It's meant for garbage collection, not conversation! And if those conversations in the dark cavern of the dumbwaiter shaft were her mother's idea of fun now, well then, she had nothing in common with her own mother.

CHAPTER EIGHT

"We're invited to cousin Hannah's house next Sunday," her father casually announced at dinner one evening.

"Who?" asked Rochelle, reaching across Marcia for the water.

"Cousin Hannah. You know her. They just bought a house in New Jersey and they want to have us over for a barbecue. They say they have a nice backyard."

"So they want to show off their house, and invited us?" offered Rochelle. Is she becoming like me? Marcia wondered.

"Maybe they actually want to see us. Did you ever think of that?" snarled her father. Marcia could see him eyeing his two daughters, frustration at their little rebellions bubbling in his guts. "Anyway, we are going."

"Anyway, have a good time." Marcia realized the words were out of her mouth and not just in her head. Her father's fist slammed down on the table, rattling the silverware.

"Don't even think you are staying here, either of you. We are all going. I am not going to insult one of the few relatives I have left."

"And you don't want to leave Marcia alone with her darling Gus," Rochelle taunted, nudging Marcia's shoulder. Marcia shoved her back.

"Enough! We are all going Sunday! It's a family trip. That's that!"

"In my day, I would never turn down a chance to see any cousin," mused her mother, placing a forkful of meatloaf daintily into her mouth as she stared into the distance.

"All your relatives lived right near you in the little shtetl, didn't they?" asked Marcia. "So it wasn't a day-long trip."

"Even still," said her mother, lost in thought. And you were younger than 19 then, Marcia thought. No comparison.

Later that evening, Marcia approached her mother. Something about the mention of New Jersey was lodged in the back of her mind.

"Where in New Jersey does Hannah live? Do you have the name of the town?"

"New Jersey's New Jersey," her mother said, waving her wet hands over the sink. "I have the address in my bag. Go look for it."

Matawan, New Jersey. It sounded familiar. Marcia would check at the school library after her classes the following day. She enjoyed looking things up. Maybe she should go into some kind of research work, she thought.

And she was good at finding what she was seeking. There it was, the little town of Matawan, New Jersey.

"I am absolutely NOT going to any house in Matawan, New Jersey!" she announced the following day, bursting into the apartment. "Read this!" She thrust some papers at her mother, pages she had mimeographed at the library.

"What's this, Marcia? I'm not going to sit and read this! Tell me what you are carrying on about!"

Marcia knew she was being mean by handing her mother several mimeographed pages. While her mother had learned to speak English well, she had never become comfortable reading it.

"Fine! I'll tell you what it says! There are several articles here about something that once happened in *Matawan, New Jersey*! A shark attack!"

"A what?"

"A shark attack! And not in the ocean near a beach! Oh, of course, they've had those at the Jersey shore. But this was different. An actual shark appeared in a creek in this little town of Matawan! So I am not going there! And you probably shouldn't either!" Marcia slammed her papers down on the kitchen table and marched off to her room.

A few hours later, after Marcia's father had come home and the family had eaten a silent dinner, Eliot called to speak to Marcia. Of course, she mumbled, shuffling toward the phone, they had called him to complain about her. *He's supposed to get me to toe the line, when he's off being free somewhere else.*

"Hi, Marsh," he began. "What's up?"

"You know what's up, I presume," she grumbled.

He sighed. "I know it's not easy for you. I was afraid of this."

"Afraid of what?"

"That they wouldn't treat you the same way they treated me when I was at Brooklyn College. Giving me the freedom I had, staying off my case."

"Because I'm a girl and you're a guy?"

"They're old school, remember. From a different world, a different culture. And they're protective of daughters."

"How understanding of you."

He sighed again. "Dad read me some of that material about the shark attack. That happened in 1916!"

"What difference does that make? The same creek that somehow connected to the ocean is still there!"

"I'm sure they closed off the connection after that. There haven't been any sharks there since 1916, right?"

"How do I know? Maybe that's just coincidence and it could happen again!"

"Our cousins do not live on a creek. They live in a house, on a residential street. It's perfectly safe."

Eliot's assurances dug deeper into Marcia's head. "I'm not going, and that's that. I don't feel that it's safe."

Another sigh. "Don't you realize why they want you and Rochelle to come with them?"

"To torment us?"

"You're so hard on Dad. They're jealous. Especially Dad. His cousin – a *younger* cousin, who immigrated to this country around the same time he did, can afford to buy a house, and Dad is still renting an apartment. The cousin is financially more successful than he is."

"So what? Who cares about a house?"

"Oh, Marcia. They all care about succeeding, about making it in America. So by bringing you and Rochelle, Mom and Dad can show up this cousin in a different way."

"Yeah? How?"

"They became successful in business and can afford a house in the suburbs. But their kids are screw-ups. One went through a nasty divorce, and the other dropped out of school and is just hanging around, floundering. So they can arrive with their two pretty daughters, one a college student, the other president of the Math League in her high school."

"So we're pawns in their little game, their competition. Great."

"Marcia, I hate seeing you so angry. Try to have a little compassion for Dad, understand what he's going through. Neither of them got to go through the rebellious phase with their parents. And you are obviously a mature young woman now, no longer a little girl. It's frightening to them, especially to Dad. Will you give him a break, little sister?"

"Nice try," she said to her parents after she hung up. "But I'm still not going."

Her stubbornness increased as the week wore on. The day of the planned drive to New Jersey, Marcia flew out of the apartment early and stayed away all day. She knew they would make her pay but she didn't care. It had become a personal crusade.

That evening, when they returned, everyone was subdued. Marcia was in her room when Rochelle came in. "So how was it?" she asked her sister.

Rochelle shrugged. "It was okay. No big deal. Kind of boring." She plopped down on her bed.

Her parents, who both seemed grumpy upon returning, said nothing to her, and she said nothing to them. Life went on. The day was not mentioned. It seemed all of them were glad it was over.

CHAPTER NINE

When Marcia landed a part-time job in the payroll office at the college, she found a measure of additional freedom. Not only did she have some money of her own to spend, but she could always say she was going in to work, since the hours were always changing. The job was totally routine, and she relished that. Gus would come in to say hello every so often, as did Natalie. But the job was all hers, no one sharing it with her. The older women basically ignored her, which she didn't mind.

Being the only student working in the office, she was often privy to conversations among the women secretaries there, conversations she wished she did not have to hear. One day, one of the women asked the others what to get her nephew for a high school graduation gift. He was going off to college, so she thought a typewriter would be a good idea.

"Nah," said the head secretary. "He'll find a girlfriend to type his papers." The others nodded. Not one of them thought to ask her, the college student in their midst, what she thought. When her shift was over, she slid out the door and headed for her science class, irritation squeezing her chest.

When she told Gus later, he laughed. "What do you care about what they think? Forget it!" She wished she could be like him. Laid-back could never be her style, she supposed.

"Eliot's moving back!" Marcia's parents were beaming that evening.

"Really?"

"He called a little while ago. He got into the graduate chemistry program at NYU and will start there in September!"

Marcia knew he'd been applying to grad schools all over the country and was surprised he'd be back in New York. Was his return a way of saying he'd been wrong to go away? Nah. Nothing to do with that. Her parents, Marcia was sure, expected him to move back home, but Marcia believed, even hoped, he would get a place in the city, near the school. He probably had money saved from his job in Atlanta. Why would she hope for that? It would validate some belief for her, something about not going backwards but always going forward. And she could visit him in New York!

Her head pounded the following day in the library. Why oh why had she picked this topic? Was she trying to ruin her joy over Eliot's imminent return? Out of all the possible topics available for the term paper in Twentieth Century European History, she had to pick the Holocaust. It was as if she had no choice – the topic just reached out of the pages of history and grabbed both her hands and would not let go. Hours in the college library taking notes on the details of atrocities was giving her a giant headache. I'm not the one who needs to know this, she told herself, as she delved deeper, determined to uncover even more examples of the perversity of those perpetrating the evil. Any little nobody suddenly had power to harm others, to feel invincible. And all the other little nobodies kept their heads down and kept on walking, hoping to be spared. Maybe they couldn't be blamed.

The photographs were especially unnerving. She photocopied away, planning to include some in her paper. The numbers, of course, were staggering, as she knew they would be. It did not seem possible, or real. No wonder there were deniers all over the place. She felt her heart rate speeding up, anger and bile rising within her. She would have to stop soon; she feared she would be ill. The words on the pages began to blur and she closed her eyes and put her head down.

"Hey! You okay?" Someone was shaking her shoulder. She sat up and stared at the reference librarian's wrinkled button-down shirt, the blue color faded nearly to a dirty white. She raised her eyes to his face. "Yeah, I'm fine."

"We're closing in 15 minutes." He pointed to the jumble of books spread out around her, including the one on which she had been resting her head. "You have to turn those in."

Obviously, she knew that. What time was it anyway? Almost 11 p.m. Hmm. She'd been at it for hours.

The dreams started that night. Of course. Even though she hadn't had nightmares in a while, picking that topic was asking for it. Was she testing herself? Or was she simply a masochist?

No, she decided. She was interested in the topic – that was it. And she was majoring in history, planning to teach on the high school level. If other history teachers could not be trusted to teach the Holocaust properly, as she suspected, then she needed to be prepared to do that. It had to be done. It was her sacred duty, her mission.

She remembered her own experience back in high school English, when they were reading *The Canterbury Tales*. When the class got up to the Nun's Prioress's Tale, that anti- Semitic rant about Jews killing Christian children on Passover and drinking their blood, the teacher dismissed it as a reflection of the thinking of the times. Okay, thought Marcia. But then someone in the class – some boy sitting in the back, she recalled – asked how we know it *wasn't* true. Since the majority of the class was Jewish, they all turned and stared at him, one of the kids yelling out, "What is wrong with you, man? You actually believe this crap?"

The kid had persisted. "Well, where's the proof it *didn't* happen?"

"Where's the proof it *did*?"

The bell had rung and the troublemaker from the back of the room smiled smugly as he gathered his stuff and slouched out the door. The teacher was long gone. Marcia was fighting an urge in her throat as she felt her lunch making its insidious way up her esophagus. This is what people in Europe believed, and no logic could change their minds. What a frightening thought, to grow up surrounded by those who harbored such beliefs. She was lucky, here in the United States, sheltered in this Brooklyn school in this mostly Jewish neighborhood, with just this one jerk in the mix.

She remained at her seat, breathing deeply, and found some gum in her bag to chew, which helped. The room had emptied and she remained at her desk for a while. That boy was a product of a Catholic school before coming to the public high school. Everyone knew that because the English teacher was always complimenting him on his perfect grammar, and he always said that the nuns made them diagram sentences, which public schools did not require, and that had drummed correct grammar into him. So I guess perfect grammar isn't the only thing that's been drummed into him, she thought, making her way, finally, out the door to her next class. She would be late, but no one would care. The Honors students were given a lot of leeway at the school.

It had been mid-April of her junior year. The English teacher had told the class that he was beginning *The Canterbury Tales* in April because the Prologue clearly states that it is April and the flowers are blooming when the *Tales* open. Instead of sunny, spring-like weather, however, they'd been having lots of rain. Fitting, Marcia thought, because the murder of Martin Luther King Jr. a few weeks earlier had cast a pall over everyone. There was much discussion in classes of the values King stood for, particularly non-violent protest, and there was much re-playing of his "I Have A Dream" speech on television and radio.

A beautiful dream, expressed so powerfully and movingly, she mused whenever she heard it. Some of the kids were memorizing sections of it. But would that ever come to be? Surrounded by hate and by ignorance, who could believe that would happen? Suddenly, all the white kids were faced with the anger of the Blacks at the school. "You just wait! It'll be a long summer!" some of them yelled in the hallways. Are they threatening us? What did *we* do? While the white kids wondered, the anger among the Black kids festered, erupting on a regular basis.

"King's tactics didn't work," one Black in her Honors history class, Len, tried to explain. "So now we feel something more forceful than nonviolence is needed."

This frightened everyone. "But then King's message is being ignored," someone pointed out during one heated discussion. "If he's being honored as a hero, his message should be followed, right?"

Marcia could sense Len's frustration. "What King was fighting for has not been accomplished. Or haven't you noticed?" he shot back. "We're not going to wait forever! So look out!"

This did not sound like the Len they knew. Then again, Marcia realized, maybe none of us ever really knew him. Just because he was smart and hard-working and fit in with the rest of the Honors kids, playing the part he had to with them, that didn't mean he wasn't nurturing an inner part of himself he'd hidden. They probably had no idea what things were like for him.

The teacher, Mr. Simon, just let them all vent for a while, his expression impassive, before telling them they were now returning to the curriculum. Marcia wondered where he stood on this issue. He never expressed any opinion other than admiration for Dr. King. His elbows covered in chalk, he strode to the blackboard and began writing names and dates relating to World War 1 in even columns. Everyone sighed and took out their notebooks to copy his list. We're so well-behaved, Marcia observed, looking around. No one is arguing with him to let the conversation – or rather, dispute – continue. It surely can't be like this in every school.

But the anger fomenting among the school's Black population clouded over the classrooms and hallways for the remainder of the term, despite all the teachers' attempts to corral the classes to moving on. Was a coldness developing between the white and Black students, those who had been friends or friendly acquaintances before? It seemed to be, Marcia realized, though it was subtle enough that everyone could pretend nothing had changed. When Marcia passed Len in the halls, she felt he avoided meeting her eyes or greeting her. She saw him with other Black students, students who were not in the Honors classes. She'd been on group projects with him and he was as nice as could be – smart, clever, funny. But now he was a stranger. A sadness, a sense of foreboding, an empathy mingled with confusion, filled her chest.

Remembering that day in such vivid detail weighed Marcia down. Then, later that year, near the end of the term, came the assassination of Robert Kennedy shortly after he'd announced that he would run for President. What a year that was! What bad luck that Kennedy family had! Why did things happen like that, in clusters? Was there any connection between those two events years ago and the research she was conducting now for this paper on the Holocaust? No, no connection, she nervously concluded. Totally different types of events. Except it nagged at her, that there might be some connection. Could it only be, she wondered glumly, that both are examples of the depths of depravity to which the human race could sink? Was she doomed to live her life in constant awareness of the horribleness that takes place in the world? A dispiriting thought.

CHAPTER TEN

H er mother had her head in the damn dumbwaiter again when Marcia got home. She heard her aunt's voice echoing through the chute, and her mother's laughing response. Was she imagining that her mother was sticking her head into that opening further and further each time? It seemed that only the lower part of her back was now visible. And how come her father or Rochelle never seemed bothered by this?

She headed straight for her room and closed the door, dumping her books on the bed. Rochelle was curled up on her bed, asleep, her math textbook open beside her. Marcia smiled. A nap seemed like a welcome idea. She curled up as well.

A strange sound was emanating from the depths of the dumbwaiter. "What's that?" her mother said to her aunt, and her aunt stopped talking. "Strange," her aunt commented. "We've never heard sounds like that here before."

Because you've been too busy talking, Marcia wanted to point out. But since it was a dream, she knew she couldn't tell them anything. They waited, peering downward into the darkness. A sloshing sound filtered upward, as if water was collecting down there. Water? There should not be water in the dumbwaiter, unless there'd been a leak somewhere and it was getting flooded.

Come inside! Marcia yelled inside her head. Her mother and aunt, however, were so fascinated by this phenomenon that they kept staring down into the depths, wondering aloud what it could be. And suddenly, they knew. A huge animal, as big as a whale, rose up out of the water, shrieking some kind of sound, and then splashed down again. Her mother and aunt both screamed at the same time and slammed shut their dumbwaiter doors.

Marcia's heart was pounding when she sat up in bed. Rochelle was no longer in the room. Daytime dreams, she had read somewhere, are scarier than nighttime dreams. She would have to avoid daytime napping. In the bathroom, she threw water on her face and stared into the mirror. Could anyone tell by looking at her? Could they tell that she had horrible dreams and crazy fears? Or did she look normal?

She then inched her way through the hallway, checking that the dumbwaiter door was closed, and peeked into the kitchen, where her mother stood at the stove, humming while stirring something in a pot. Rochelle sat at the table, working on math homework. She was so good in math, a subject Marcia barely tolerated.

It's this apartment, she decided. This family here. That is what is doing this to her. One day, she would get away, move somewhere else, have her own place. A place without a dumbwaiter, for sure. Right then and there, she made the decision not to go directly to graduate school but to get a job right after college graduation, a job with a salary that would allow her to move out. It was her only chance. She could always attend grad school evenings, or, if she went into teaching as she planned, during the summers. It was still a few years away, but she realized the importance of this decision.

They would fight her on it, she knew. That was looked down upon. You moved out when you got married. It was different for a girl. Eliot's move to Atlanta was accepted both because he was male and was living with roommates. They worried about him but they accepted it. It would not be the same, she knew, but she would not be deterred. Let them carry on and worry and wring their hands over what it would look like. She would do it. That was that.

Feeling lighter because of her resolve, she called Gus and arranged to meet him at his friend's apartment. Hey, maybe something would be available in that very building. The possibilities were appealing.

She couldn't believe she was so comfortable going to this guy's apartment, this Benny guy, someone she wasn't even friends with and didn't really know. But Gus said it would be all right and it always seemed to be. His friends were as laid-back as he was. The apartment was like a communal motel, with everyone coming and going. At least ten people, including Gus, had the key. He ought to charge for this, Marcia often thought. Maybe living alone is not really what he likes; maybe he likes the constant camaraderie, the feeling that he's still a kid, not a working adult. She knew when she had her own place, she would most likely relish the aloneness.

A few of them were sitting on the floor, eating a pizza and passing a joint. She declined to join them, saying she'd wait for Gus. One couple left early for an antiwar demonstration. They had signs leaning against the wall and they retrieved them and exited, waving. At least they aren't trying to convince the rest of the group to join them.

When Gus arrived, he hugged and kissed her, then plopped down on the floor with the others, pulling her down with him. When the pizza was gone and some of them started strumming their guitars and singing "Blowin' In The Wind," which Marcia had been hearing in her sleep already, a few of them just stretched out on the floor and went to sleep. Gus took her hand and led her into the bedroom, where he closed the door behind them.

That's all it took for Marcia to feel calm when she headed home later that night. Maybe I am a loose woman after all. She laughed at that expression, 'loose woman.' She did feel kind of loose-limbed climbing the steps to the apartment. Maybe loose is better than tight, its opposite. She smiled at that concept.

A door slammed as she passed the third floor in her building, and Marcia started, reaching for the wall. When she saw a young couple exiting their apartment, dressed as if for an evening out, she nodded and they nodded back. As they passed her on their way down the stairs, Marcia caught a whiff of the woman's flowery, lavender-like perfume. Her heart continued pounding as they walked past her and as she pushed herself away from the wall. Just hearing a door slam unexpectedly while lost in reverie and she momentarily freaked. She had to stay more aware, she realized as she ran the rest of the way upstairs.

CHAPTER ELEVEN

Why did she feel drawn to the beach? Was she like a homing pigeon? She never even went in the water; she just sat on a blanket or beach chair and watched. What kept her interest? Nothing in particular. The water and the way it could change, from calm to rough and back again. The shoreline changing as the water inched up further, or inched back, depending on the time of day. The way people behaved at the beach. Showing off their perfect bodies in their sexy bathing suits, laughing loudly for show, shrieking as the waves hit them, tossing Frisbees and volleyballs to appear carefree and fun-loving. She knew she was judging everyone harshly, assuming their motives were self-serving, but she believed she was correct in her judgments.

"You're going yourself?" Rochelle had asked when she saw Marcia packing up her beach bag. "I wish I was finished with school for the year already, like you are. I'd go too." Marcia didn't answer. She wanted to go herself, to be by herself. That was something Rochelle would never choose. Her little sister, now 14 and in high school, seemed to have a lot of friends. Marcia suspected she had a boyfriend but was keeping that well-hidden. Well, they were different. Marcia wondered why people have such a hard time believing that she liked going places herself and being by herself sometimes. Did everyone else have such a strong need to be surrounded by others? A need she did not share? Throwing sunscreen and a book into her bag, she zipped it shut and headed out.

The little kids were cute. They weren't yet aware of other people seeing them. One little girl caught her eye, playing in the sand not far from her perch. Her young parents were sitting nearby, chatting amiably with each other while watching their daughter, sipping from cans of soda.

The little girl, wearing a red and white polka dotted two piece bathing suit, with straps that kept slipping off her little shoulders, was busy, totally immersed in some project. She seemed to be building something in the sand, something that involved little plastic figurines and a few Lego blocks, obviously brought from home.

"What are you making, Bianca?" the father asked. Marcia guessed the child's age at two.

"It's a secret," declared the little girl, and the parents laughed. The girl's sunhat, a white ruffled affair, slipped sideways on her head and she righted it quickly. She stopped and thought for a moment, then took a little green shovel from her arsenal of toys and carved a circle around her in the sand, enclosing her, her project, and her pail of supplies within the circle.

"What are you doing, honey?" asked the young mother. She was attractive, with long, straight blonde hair in a pony tail and a black bikini gracing her well-toned frame. She probably works out to that Jack Lalanne exercise show on TV while her daughter is napping or in nursery school, Marcia decided.

The girl did not answer for a while. Marcia thought she was deliberately ignoring her parents but she was concentrating, her pert little face showing her intensity with its furrowed brow and set lips. Apparently, she was simply biding her time as she considered her answer.

"This is my house," she declared, pointing at the circle. "No one can come in." The parents laughed. Obviously, they got a kick out of their little darling, their precocious baby. Marcia was fascinated by the child. Encircling herself and her castle. Protecting herself. Let's see what happens next.

She was not disappointed. At some point, Marcia knew, the parents would want to come into the girl's circle. "Come on, honey, let's go down to the water now," said the mother, rising from her chair. It was then that Marcia noticed a tiny belly above the bikini bottom and realized the mother was probably pregnant. Ah, the perfect family in the making. The mother rubbed her belly absently for a moment, then stepped toward her daughter.

"No! You can't come in here!" the little girl yelled. Again, her ruffly hat slipped down over one eye and she angrily shoved it back up.

Both parents laughed. "Don't you want to go in the water with Mommy?" asked the dad. "It's hot. You can get wet…"

The girl pushed her mother's feet back. "Out of my circle!" She set her little heart-shaped mouth in a pout.

"Can *I* come into your circle?" asked the dad, looking at his wife with a wink.

"No! No one can!" She re-drew the line where her mother's foot had smudged it, and bent back to her project.

"Okay, then," said the mother. "I'll go get wet all by myself." Walking away slowly, looking back every few steps as if expecting her daughter to come running after her, the mother headed toward the water.

The girl did not react. She was working intently on whatever it was she was creating, her head bent low. Marcia was entranced.

The father studied his daughter. "What are you building there?" he asked.

"I'm not telling."

Marcia wanted to applaud this little girl.

"You won't tell me what you're building?" he said. "Can I visit you there when it's finished and you move in?"

The girl stopped and thought. "Maybe," she said. "I'll have to see." Good for you, thought Marcia. The father burst out laughing. Shaking his head, he returned to the paperback he was reading.

Marcia knew she would remember this little family scene. How did this child know? Where did she get the confidence to create her boundary and protect it? Was she, Marcia, ever like that child? Could she aspire to be that way now? Or was it too late?

The mother returned, shaking water over her husband and daughter, laughing gaily. The father shook the droplets out of his hair but the little girl threw her mother a condescending look.

"Stop, Mommy!" she commanded, holding out a pudgy little hand. "*Me* decide – no water here!" The mother, chuckling, shrugged and grabbed a towel.

It did not seem as if any of them had noticed her, but Marcia began to feel like a peeping Tom. She gathered up her things to leave.

"You're getting sand all over the floor," Marcia's mother pointed out when she got home. "And I just mopped today."

"Sorry. I'll clean it up after my shower."

"I see a sunburn already on your shoulders. Why didn't you use sunscreen?"

"I did. I guess I couldn't reach back there."

"Gus couldn't put sunscreen on your back for you?"

Marcia closed the bathroom door. "He didn't come with me. I went myself," she yelled through the door. She couldn't wait for them to ask where Gus had been hiding these last few weeks, so she could tell them he'd dropped out of school and left New York, for horizons unknown. They would feel vindicated, and she could stoke her anger further.

Standing beneath the hot water, which did burn when it hit her shoulders and back, she realized that that was all right. He was living his own life, doing his thing. She didn't care.

She was grateful he'd still been around the summer before, which had ended with the massacre of 11 Israeli athletes at the Munich Olympics. His hugs gave her comfort during that time as did his silent support for her grief and fear. He was good at that.

Her parents, sensing Marcia's level of fear and paranoia, talked about Mark Spitz whenever news of the Munich Massacre, as it had been dubbed, came on. Their desperate attempt to shift the focus made Marcia wince.

"He's Jewish," her mother crowed. "And he won seven gold medals! He broke records! Amazing! And the whole world sees that. That's progress." It was as if he were her child. In a sense, he represented something to her, a giant Fuck You to those terrorists and to the German country.

Marcia just shook her head. "You do realize that American security whisked him out of Germany after those terrorists got there. Because he's Jewish, they thought he would be in danger. Israeli athletes murdered, on German soil. That's progress?" Her parents stared after her as she left the room.

After that, the photo of the masked terrorist on the roof of the Israeli compound appeared in every newspaper and television news program. She saw that picture behind her eyelids when she went to bed. We have to be constantly on alert, she concluded, constantly fearful and wary. It is never over. Never.

"I got the job!" she announced to Natalie later in the week at the student coffee shop where they'd planned to meet. It was more empty than usual in the summer. "Congratulations!" Natalie engulfed her in a hug.

"The school you wanted?"

"Yup."

"You'll tell me how the interview went so I'll be prepared for one I've got next week."

"The chairman was perfectly nice. He did not ask any trick questions."

"I should be so lucky."

"You will be." She patted her friend's arm.

"Guess what, everyone!" Her parents and Rochelle were at the kitchen table eating dinner. The all looked up at her expectantly.

"I got a job!"

"Oh, that's wonderful! We're so proud of you!" Both her parents got up and hugged her and Rochelle gave her a thumbs up.

"Just graduated college a few weeks ago and a job already!" exclaimed her father, beaming. "You'll call your grandparents later and tell them yourself."

"Sure," she said. Even that directive failed to irritate her. She was on the way to a grown-up life, to freedom.

CHAPTER TWELVE

Weeks later, it was time to break the news. The real news. She took a deep breath before walking into the living room, where her parents were on the couch, her father reading the paper, her mother knitting something blue. The TV – still a black and white, as her parents refused to indulge in a color television when the one they had was working fine – was playing some musical event in the background, a conductor waving his arms around as an orchestra obeyed.

"Hello, dear," said her mother without looking up. Her father looked over his bifocals and nodded. "Did you have a nice time with Natalie?"

"Yes, very nice." She stood in the doorway for a few minutes and then headed for the armchair facing the couch. "Actually, I have some very exciting news." She decided to just say it quickly, get it over with. "I took an apartment."

The silence, Marcia noted, had a sound. The sound of a heavy thud, the sound of a deep inhale and a held breath, the sound of dead trees in a lonely winter forest. That was the sound that greeted her announcement.

"It's not far," she blabbered on. "And I'll have a really easy commute to work, just two subway stops."

The silence thundered.

Finally, it broke. "You didn't tell us you were looking at apartments," her mother said in a small, confused voice.

"I waited until I had one to tell you." She didn't say that she was putting off the argument that would have ensued had she revealed her plan. She'd carried that plan within her like a secret jewel for weeks. Now it was a fact, a done deal, and no one could change it. Had she been afraid they would have managed to stop her, to change her mind? Her determination to be free of family, of everyone and everything, was too strong. But still.

"The school where you'll be working is so close to here," her mother went on, grasping. "And a cooked dinner is ready for you every evening. You'll have to cook for yourself in an apartment, and …"

"I know that. I'm ready, Mom. I want to try being independent."

Her father was glaring at her. "Yourself? In an apartment? Why didn't you at least get a roommate? A girlfriend?"

"This is what I want. No one else to worry about or to bother me."

"To worry about?" echoed her mother. "You worry about us? We bother you?" It sounded like she was about to cry.

Marcia sighed. "That's not what I mean. I tell you what, Mom. I will need some pots and pans, some cheap dishes and cutlery. Why don't you come shopping with me over the weekend? You can help me pick out stuff."

"You will be able to afford the rent?" her father barked. "And other expenses? Utilities, and groceries?"

"I figured everything out. The building is rent-controlled. It will be within my budget." She did not tell them that her figuring revealed that it would be tight, but she was willing to live on a tight budget. Her wild desperation to be on her own, to be free, was driving her. If she had to eat plain spaghetti or canned tuna every night, that would be fine.

"Are you sure the building is safe? The neighborhood?"

It was a neighborhood considered "borderline," but Marcia didn't care. She would get ten locks on the door, if she had to. "It's safe," she said. "I checked it out."

"I'm very excited, actually," she said to the two stunned people staring at her from the couch. "This is the beginning of my adulthood." The concert on TV was apparently over, and applause sounded faintly in the room.

"What will we tell the family?" her mother nearly whispered. "Moving into a place of your own? That's only supposed to happen when you get married."

"Things are different now. We're not in Europe, in a shtetl. Can you trust me on this, and not give me a hard time?" She stood up.

They were in shock, and did not answer. Sighing, Marcia stood up.

"What about…furniture? A bed?" Her father had spoken.

"I am saving money from my summer job to get a few things I'll need. I'll start with just basics, then get more along the way." She didn't care if she slept on the floor or ate standing up as long as she was on her own, in her own little place.

"Usually, parents get their daughter a bedroom set when she gets married," her mother mused. Marcia looked down at them, and was filled with pity. They were confused. They did not know what to do. This was not in their playbook.

"Do not be concerned," she said. "We can worry about all that stuff in the future. I will handle what I need now." Before the discussion could drag on any further, Marcia left the room. Let them mull it over, she thought. I don't have to stand there and watch.

The following evening, her mother called Marcia to the phone and then disappeared down the hallway. "So, sis! Hear you dropped a bomb on Mom and Dad last night!"

"Word travels fast, doesn't it? They called you to complain about me already?"

Eliot chuckled. Marcia could just see him lounging on his sofa, his feet up on the coffee table, cradling his phone while watching something on TV. The color TV he and his roommates had purchased. "I wouldn't say complain, exactly. You just threw them for a loop, that's all. They never expected you to move out so quickly."

"You mean before getting married?"

"Marcia, Marcia, Marcia. You need to calm down. They'll get used to the idea."

"Whether they get used to it or not doesn't matter. It's what I'm doing."

"Why do you have so much hostility in you? You always sound like you're bursting with anger. Where's it coming from?"

"What are you now, a shrink?"

"Hey, don't attack me. I'm on your side."

"Did you even tell them that you're taking an apartment in New York when you come back? Or do they still believe you'll move back home?"

"Well,…"

"Ha. So don't go lecturing me."

"I'm just suggesting you go easy on them. That's all. Their darling little girl is growing up, and growing away from them. Imagine how difficult that must be."

"Since *you* are so full of sympathy and understanding, I don't have to be. You can make up for me so I can just focus on my plans and my future. I can be the selfish one. Is there a problem with that?"

Eliot sighed loudly. "Okay, I give up. At least promise you'll invite me for dinner at your apartment!"

Marcia laughed. "Absolutely. Only you'll have to bring the pizza!"

She went back to her secret park regularly that summer. She thought of it as her secret even though it was just a park, which had a track for running. The track wound around a lake and a café and a playground and a doggie play area. She ran and ran, in spite of the summer heat, soaking up the sights of the parents with their little children in strollers, of the paddle boats out on the lake, of the friends and couples leaving the café together, of dogs of all sizes pulling their owners along on leashes as they panted and drooled.

She'd received the curriculum guidelines from her new department head. The social studies department seemed to be very organized. Every day, she went over more of the material, even the material for the classes she would not be teaching. She wanted to know how they divided up the historical periods covered, which grades got stuck with which wars.

She was glad to see that she would have a variety of classes. Two freshmen, one sophomore, and two junior. She figured only the really experienced teachers got to teach seniors. She was curious about what those grades would be reading in their English classes. It would be ideal if there could be some coordination between the two departments in that regard, but she was not naïve – she knew how unlikely that would be in a large city high school. Every department protected its turf and resented being expected to consider any other department's concerns.

Marcia laughed as she ran. That was all right. She'd be all right. Whatever the situation into which she would be thrust, she would adapt. She'd be so happy to be in the grown-up world at last that she would handle this job, whatever it involved. Student teaching had shown her that she could be a very effective teacher. She had been sent to a school with a rather tough reputation for student teaching, and she'd done well. The kids had respected her, on the whole. So she could do this. Most importantly, she would have her very own place to come home to after work, with no one asking her questions or judging her mood or eyeing her suspiciously. She'd be on her own. So even if some of the kids gave her a hard time or if department rules or paperwork got to her, it would be fine. She had an apartment.

Finished with the run one day, she plopped onto a bench and withdrew a water bottle from her backpack. Sweat was dripping down her face and her back. It felt good in the heat.

"Hey," said a husky voice. Marcia looked up and saw a muscular, dark-haired guy, in sunglasses and a black tank top. Also sweating. "Mind if I sit here?" He pointed to the empty spot beside her on the bench.

"No problem," she responded, scooting over to the edge of the bench a bit, to give him more room. He smiled at her as he sat down. He wiped his head and neck with a small towel and extracted a water bottle from somewhere – she couldn't see from where. She watched him tip his head back and slurp the water. Then they began to talk.

He was a few years older than Marcia and worked in a bank, hoping to move up the ranks and build a career there. He seemed interested in what Marcia would be teaching as he said he always enjoyed history in school. He said he just started jogging again after he'd been laid up with a broken ankle, and he lived near the park. He pointed vaguely down the street.

They parted amicably, wishing each other good luck and laughing about possibly seeing each other jogging again. Marcia felt buoyant and light on the bus ride home. She looked out the window, noting the birds flitting through the trees and the children running through the fire hydrants spouting water. He'd been nice, she'd been nice, and they had had a friendly, casual conversation. She was capable of that. It was, she believed, all part of the new life on which she was about to embark.

CHAPTER THIRTEEN

She dressed carefully for her first department meeting. Well, it wasn't actually an official department meeting, the chairman had told her, since school was out and the teachers were not required to come in until September. However, a few who were working on some projects for the chairman would be there and he thought it would be nice for her to meet them and receive some guidance before the term began.

The old building was not air-conditioned and it was summer, so she selected her sleeveless green dress with the belted waist. It wasn't too short, she decided, studying herself in the full-length mirror. It was professional, suitable.

Entering the school building while it was so empty seemed creepy. A guard had been alerted to let her in and she noticed he had a clipboard listing those who were coming in that day. Apparently, various members of the staff came in over the summer for various, mysterious reasons. A musty smell filled the hallways, a mixture of pent-in heat, bleach, and perhaps the memories of all those active teenage hormones that had been floating around in those areas so recently.

She opened the door to the social studies office and was greeted by the sight of five teachers and the chairman, all wearing shorts and sitting around a large conference table, talking and laughing and helping themselves to cookies arrayed on a plate in the center of the table and cans of soda sitting in a cooler on the floor. A mimeograph machine rested on a table in the corner, and Marcia was certain she could smell the pungent ink from the doorway.

They stopped and quieted when she entered, looking her up and down. Then one woman rose. "You must be our newest acquisition," she said, extending her hand. "I am Celia. Welcome to our crazy little world!"

After introductions were made all around and Marcia was invited to sit and join their "party," she learned that quite a bit of camaraderie existed in the department. They all offered to help her with anything, to come to them with any questions or problems, and to promise to attend their annual Christmas party. She relaxed immediately.

At some point, the chairman insisted they provide Marcia with a sense of what she could expect at the beginning of the term.

"DO NOT, under any circumstance," said Celia, "accept cafeteria patrol."

Seeing her bewildered expression, the others explained. Everyone gets assigned one period of school duty, and cafeteria patrol is the worst.

"Although I lost quite a bit of weight when I had it," joked Lena, an older woman sitting across from Marcia, with wavy gray hair and a tinkly laugh. "I completely lost my appetite for that entire term, could barely eat."

"It's no fun," added Rodney. "And they try to stick it to the newbies. Which is pretty dumb, actually, because that is no way to hold on to new teachers. I think we lost a few that way."

"What – do the kids have food fights?" Marcia asked.

"All kinds of fights. It's where they let loose. Only the male gym teachers take it without complaining."

"You just come to me if you get that assignment," the chairman assured her. He smiled reassuringly. "Don't worry. I'll get it traded for something less…"

"Disgusting," Rodney threw in. Another man whose name Marcia forgot nodded sagely.

"Like..?" Marcia asked. She was getting nervous. Maybe this was more than she could handle. Maybe the kids would be awful and she would not be able to control them.

"Oh, hallway patrol, or study hall. Something like that."

"Don't scare our poor rookie," scolded Celia, apparently reading Marcia's mind. "The kids here are good in class. It's only the cafeteria that brings out the worst in them."

"We should let them go out during their lunch periods," mused Rodney, adjusting his glasses.

"Then they'd never come back!" declared the other man.

"That's the idea," said Rodney, to a round of laughter.

The chairman, Robert Price, took her on a tour of the building. He was courtly and businesslike. His brown mustache looked like it required a great deal of care and Marcia tried not to stare at it when she looked at him. It was so neat and well trimmed that she decided it represented the man himself, the persona he wished to present.

Opening every door for her, he showed her the rooms used by the social studies department, the study halls, the main office where teachers clocked in and out and where he demonstrated the clocking procedure, the deans' offices, the principal's office, the library, the teachers' cafeteria, and then the dreaded student cafeteria. Marcia took in the cavernous space, imagining the students screaming and yelling and fighting and throwing food. She thought she could even smell the sickening smell of institutional food slopped onto aluminum trays. She shivered, remembering the warning about cafeteria patrol. The yawning emptiness of the entire building seemed mocking, as if to taunt her with its quiet when it was really saying: Just you wait til September! You won't recognize this place then!

"Well, I think that's it," he concluded, shrugging. "Oh, the faculty ladies' rooms are on every floor, at either corner," he added. "And there are faculty lounges near every department office. Ours is directly opposite the office."

Marcia, overwhelmed, merely nodded. "Thank you," she said.

She walked out together with the other teachers. Robert stayed behind, doing paperwork at his desk. No one commented on Marcia's dress; she knew they understood that she thought she had to present a professional appearance.

"Listen," said Heather, putting a hand on Marcia's arm as they stepped outside. "No one mentioned this, but you should know. There are gangs in the school. They usually don't get violent, but every once in a while, you know…"

Marcia swallowed. "Uh, I'm glad you're telling me."

"If you see any fighting, call the dean's office. Don't try to break up anything yourself."

"It's a great day for the beach!" declared Celia, pulling sunglasses out of her bag, squinting in the harsh sunlight.

"I despise the beach," intoned Rodney. "Too much sand."

"You're supposed to ignore the sand, you old goat," said the other man, "and concentrate on the girls in bikinis."

"Ignore those two," whispered Lena. "They're our very own traveling road show."

Wishing one another an enjoyable summer, they parted ways. Celia slipped Marcia her phone number, in case she had any questions before September. Still jittery, Marcia did feel somewhat relieved. Maybe she could handle this after all. She had to, since she now had an apartment requiring rent payments.

Well, she told herself as she headed to the subway, there are other types of jobs out there. But she would give this her best shot.

CHAPTER FOURTEEN

"So, my darling granddaughter," said Marcia's grandfather on a visit one summer day, when Marcia made her father very happy by telling him she would visit his parents after work. Her grandfather's bushy white mustache wiggled as he smiled. "Tell us how you are doing! So much going on for you!"

Her grandmother, in an apron sporting a faded picture of the Eiffel Tower and was therefore a gift from some traveling relative, brought in a plate of her home-baked cookies, smoothed back Marcia's hair, kissed her forehead, and took a seat. "Yes!" she added, clapping her hands. "Is this summer a break for you, just working at the department store?"

"I guess," said Marcia, selecting a cookie. "But I'm also taking a course at night. Something that will go towards my Masters degree."

"You are smart, not wasting time, building your credentials like that," intoned her grandfather. "Your parents are so proud of you. What kind of course is it?"

"In the history department," she answered, munching on the cookie. "On dictatorships."

The grandparents nodded solemnly. "Ah, dictatorships," said her grandmother, almost in a whisper. "People study and study them, and they still exist." She shook her head.

"All dictatorships?" asked her grandfather. "That would be a very long course."

"Just the ones picked out for the course. Dictatorships today, not in the past." She felt compelled to include that.

"Like?" They both leaned forward, seeming to be truly interested.

"Well, now we're studying Iran."

"Hmph, Iran," said her grandfather, waving his hand. "No one cares about Iran."

After several cookies, Marcia took her leave, feeling good about the visit. Hugging her grandmother, she smelled cookie dough. Hugging her grandfather, she smelled mothballs. She waved to them as she left, realizing what a cute little couple they made. If her father didn't push so much, she knew, she would be willing to visit them more often.

From the depths of a deep sleep, she thought she heard the phone near the kitchen ringing. It must be in my dream, she decided. She tried to dream it away but it persisted. She sat bolt upright and raced into the hallway before her parents could hear the phone. It seemed they could sleep through just about anything. She sensed it was something they should not know about.

"Ma..Marsh…I need you," the whispered voice croaked.

She was wide awake now, on high alert. "Natalie?"

"Come pick me up. Please." The words seemed parsed, as if carved from a tiny wood block that only had room for the fewest possible letters.

"Where? Where are you?" Was she shouting? She would have to keep her voice down.

As Natalie checked for an address, Marcia grabbed paper and pencil. The address was in the Village, Manhattan's famed Greenwich Village. "I'll be waiting outside the building." She hung up.

As quietly as possible, Marcia rushed back to her room, where Rochelle was sleeping soundly, got dressed in the dark, then hurried out the door, closing it gently behind her. Rochelle had rolled over and mumbled something, but remained asleep, and her parents had apparently not heard anything. The only phone in the apartment was in the hallway outside the kitchen. Marcia believed she was particularly attuned to sounds from outside her room; thereby, she heard the phone and no one else did.

Unfamiliar with driving in Manhattan, it took Marcia a while to find the apartment building. The emptiness of the streets and highways helped. The eerie, early morning darkness enveloped the car in a suffocating embrace. Marcia could not wait to find her friend and get out of that area. When she pulled up in front of a nondescript old building that looked as if it had seen better days, a bedraggled looking Natalie arose from a clump on the pavement and sidled over to the passenger side, sliding in without looking at Marcia.

Marcia looked over at her, however. Her hair was a tangled mess, her face splotchy with makeup running all over it, her clothing wrinkled and dirty, and her hands were shaking. "Don't ask me anything now, please," Natalie whispered. "Let's just go."

Marcia stepped on the gas and headed back to Brooklyn. Natalie alternated between sniffling and sleeping. "Thank you," she whispered at one point.

At a red light, Marcia stole another look. Slumped in the seat, Natalie looked like a homeless woman, a drug addict, a beggar. Marcia couldn't wait to hear how she had gotten into whatever mess this was. She was also disgusted by what she saw. Had something terrible happened to her, had she been assaulted, kidnapped? Or had she chosen something dangerous, bringing this on herself? If so, how could Natalie sink to this?

When they pulled up in front of Natalie's building, Natalie opened her eyes wide. "No, no, I can't go home now. Not at this hour, not like this."

She could have mentioned this earlier, thought Marcia. "Okay, where to, then? I can take you to my…"

"Do you have the key to your own apartment yet?"

"No, not til next week." They sat in the parked car as the darkness around them slowly lifted and glimmers of sun filtered through. "I know," Marcia said, pulling out, "there's an all-night diner a few blocks away. We'll go there."

"Okay," whispered Natalie, slumping further downward.

Marcia parked next to a huge truck in the still-darkened parking lot and then practically pulled Natalie out of the car and through the diner's door, then steered her to a booth. The air conditioner was on full blast in the diner, and Marcia shivered. Two large, husky truck drivers looked over at them from their stools at the counter and then returned to their food. Natalie immediately headed to the ladies' room. Marcia ordered them both coffee and omelets, assuming her friend needed some protein as well as caffeine. When Natalie returned, she looked somewhat more composed. Sliding into the seat opposite Marcia, she sighed dramatically.

"You're waiting for the story, right?" She picked up the salt shaker and twirled it around in her fingers. Marcia held up her hands and shrugged.

"You do deserve that. Oh," she remarked when the food arrived and was placed before her, the steam rising from the plate. "You ordered for me."

"Eat something, Natalie. And drink the coffee."

"I don't have any money. My bag somehow disappeared last…"

Marcia waved her hand. "Forget that. I'm paying."

Natalie snorted. "Good old Marcia," she said. "Always sensible, always prepared. Can always be counted on to do the right thing, the helpful thing."

"If that's what I am, then it seems that's what you need right now," Marcia shot back, bristling with the insult.

"Because that's not what *I* am, right? I can always be counted on to do the stupid thing, the impulsive thing, the possibly dangerous thing. I should try to be more like you. But I don't think I'm capable."

Marcia put down her fork. "You have a lot to look forward to now, remember. You graduated. You have a job at a high school in Queens, a good school."

"Yes, in a good neighborhood, which is why I won't be able to afford my own apartment nearby."

"I thought you found someone to room with."

"I did. Haven't even met her yet. But *you'll* have your own place, and that's so much better." She stared down at her eggs, as if wondering what she was supposed to do with them.

"Oh, for goodness sake, Natalie! Are you looking for things to complain about? You'll have your independence! And a roommate might actually be a good thing for you."

"So I won't go overdosing on anything without anyone around to call an ambulance? So if I try to slit my wrists, someone will be there? That's what you're thinking, I know." She lifted the coffee cup to her lips and took a tiny sip.

Don't tell me what I'm thinking, Marcia thought, looking across at her friend and feeling the cloud of annoyance puffing up inside her chest.

"Okay, maybe it's time you told me what happened." Marcia sat back.

Natalie rubbed absently at a spot on her throat, which Marcia noticed seemed bruised. Alarmed, Marcia decided then and there that no matter how upset she ever became over anything, she would never, *never* lose control. She would never, *never* allow herself to sink this low, to wind up in any kind of danger or with any suspicious person who could harm her. Never, she vowed. She straightened her spine, forcing herself to focus on Natalie's miserable, unhappy face.

"Well," Natalie began, suddenly taking an interest in her omelet and slowly slicing a piece and placing it daintily into her mouth, then chewing thoughtfully. "It started yesterday afternoon, around…oh…maybe three o'clock. Or maybe closer to 4…I'm not sure…"

"The exact time doesn't matter," Marcia intoned, crossing her arms. "Go on."

"Don't get mad at me, please! I couldn't take that now." Natalie put her fork down and put her head in her hands.

Marcia waited, silent, staring at the pitiable figure across from her, hoping her lip wasn't curling in disgust.

"I'm not mad at you," she finally said. "I'm worried about you." As the words emerged, she realized they were true. There had to be a way to help poor Natalie, whatever the problem was.

"My father and I got into a fight. A really big fight. He was home from work…I'm not sure why…,maybe he didn't feel well…or maybe he got fired. Again." She shook her head, looking downward. Natalie's father had an explosive temper, which had gotten him fired from a string of various jobs. He would always come home to report on how this or that boss was a total moron and had no real reason to fire him. Once, a co-worker at some store even filed charges against him for shoving him against a wall, but that went nowhere.

"So he was in a pissed-off mood. Major. And my mother wasn't home." Natalie's mother was a calming, stabilizing influence on her husband.

"So what was the fight about?" Marcia felt that if she didn't prod, the story would go no further.

"He saw that I was going out, and he demanded to know where. I mean, I graduated college, have a job lined up, and I still have to answer for where I'm going? For Christ's sake, what does it take for that to stop?"

"In their world? Being married."

"Then we'll be answering to the husband, right? From the fat into the frying pan?"

"Anyway…" prompted Marcia.

"I don't remember what I said anymore. Either: none of your fuckin' business. Or: I'm not sure. Or: I thought I'd just do some streetwalking and see what kind of business I could drum up."

"And?"

"Of course he blew up. Moved as if to slap me, but I backed away and opened the door. Fortunately, the woman in the apartment across the hall was just getting home, unlocking her door. 'Hello, dear,' she says to me, so sweetly it was like from another world. Here I've got this innocent, friendly lady on one side and my deranged father on the other. He would never scream or carry on in front of neighbors, so he shut up and just stood there, glowering. Well, when the woman went into her apartment and closed her door, he lit into me again.

"'You useless tramp!' he screams at me. "And more along those lines." Tears were now forming in Natalie's already reddened eyes. If only her mother had been at home, Marcia thought. She would have stopped this.

"And then he says what he's wanted to say to me my whole life. 'You're not anything like *her*.'"

Marcia leaned forward. "Her? Who?"

"Exactly. I slammed the apartment door shut and faced him. I demanded to know." Natalie gazed around suddenly, her eyes locking onto the little jukebox against the wall at the end of their table. Her sudden interest in the song selections displayed there, which prominently featured Bobby Rydell titles, oldies but goodies, irritated Marcia so that she grabbed Natalie's hand.

"Well? What was the answer?"

Natalie turned and stared at Marcia, her gaze glassy. "His wife."

"His…wife."

"Yes. I know I was named after someone in his family, some relative who had been killed by the Nazis, just gunned down in the street. That's all I was ever told. Turns out he was married before. And lost this first wife in a horrible, traumatic way. She was killed and her body mutilated right before his eyes." Natalie closed her own eyes.

"And he never talked about it," Marcia added. Natalie nodded.

"Of course I was exploding with a million questions. Did he have children with her? Why was this kept a secret? Was I expected to live up to this idealized woman because of my name? But he shut down. Waved me away, as if I could go and do whatever now, he didn't give a shit. I was a lost cause. He went to his bedroom and shut the door."

"And you?"

"I flew out of there like a bat out of hell. First I went to my mother's office. Well, that lawyer, her boss, was giving her dictation when I arrived, so I had to wait, pacing in the waiting room like a tiger in the zoo. I finally had a chance to be alone with her, and I broke down, crying, accusing her of keeping this big secret from me. She was so upset to see my like that. She tried to explain that it's how *he* wanted it; he just couldn't deal with talking about it, blablabla. I asked point blank if they'd had children, and she turned her head and mumbled that what difference would that make now. So there's my answer. More secrets. I am so sick of them! No wonder he's hated me my entire life, no wonder nothing I did was ever perfect enough! And my mother covering for him. It's sickening. The whole point of naming a child after someone who's dead is to honor that person's memory, right? But in this case, what did it accomplish? It was a constant reminder of a person he lost and a horrible past, not to mention a prison locking me in, a prison sentence I never understood."

Natalie was openly crying now, and her voice had grown louder. The two truck drivers had left and been replaced at the counter by two businessmen in suits and ties, despite the heat outside. Who cares who hears this, Marcia thought, taking Natalie's hand. "I'm so sorry," she whispered. "I wish you'd called me then."

Natalie nodded. "I should have. But I was so wound up, I was like one of those spring toys, ready to be launched into the atmosphere. I was just crazed. I ran out into the street, and kept running. When I got to the subway station, I raced down the steps and got onto the first train. Didn't even know where it was going til I decided to get out. And some guy got out at the same stop and was following me."

Oh no, here it comes, Marcia thought.

"He caught up with me, asked me if I wanted to go to a party with him."

Marcia simply stared across at Natalie. Just how stupid could her friend be?

"Well, I wish I could tell you more details, but the fact is, I blacked out at some point and don't remember." She swirled the straw in her water.

"Did you take any drugs?" Marcia tried to make her voice sound gentle rather than judgmental.

"Not deliberately. But they were all chugging away at this drink someone made, and I'm pretty sure it was laced with something. I felt really weird after drinking it, kind of faint and nauseous, and I found a couch to lie down on. Music was blasting and people were laughing and grabbing at each other. Next thing I know, I wake up in the hallway, outside the apartment door, on this cold cement floor."

Marcia wasn't buying it. "That's all you remember?"

"What's the difference anyway?" Natalie said angrily. "I just wanted escape! I thought I would find it there! I know, I know, it was risky and stupid. Why do I always have to be good? So they can be proud of me, and not embarrassed by me? I'm never good enough anyway! So why not go totally to the other side?! Maybe I'll actually enjoy it!"

Marcia almost asked if she'd enjoyed it so far, but refrained. Her disgust with Natalie simply deepened. Never never never will I let myself be in that kind of situation, she vowed. I will never lose my self-control, never let someone else convince me to go or do anything I don't want. This – this Natalie in front of me – is the result.

"Don't be pissed at me, Marsh," Natalie pleaded, her eyes red, her face bloated. She could manage to look like a lost little girl, Marcia noted.

"I'm worried about you," Marcia replied. "Don't do anything like this again, ok?"

"Good old Marcia, looking after immature me."

"Oh, stop that. Just learn from this and move on. You have your whole future ahead of you."

"Do you realize what my father did to me? I won't ever forgive him. He cursed me for life by naming me after his wife. I could never be her. He's hated me forever, and I never knew why! "

Marcia sighed. "You're the one who always said you don't take them seriously, you let their comments slide off your back so you can live your own life!"

"This is different!"

The waitress was hovering nearby, holding a pot of coffee, and rapidly blinking her over-mascara-ed eyes. Marcia waved her away and signaled for the check. "So where am I taking you now? Are you ready to go home? You need a hot shower and a long nap. And a shampoo, if you don't mind my saying that." Natalie's hair, her pride and joy, was dirty and greasy-looking.

Natalie actually managed a weak smile as she checked her watch. "Another half hour and they'll both be on the way to work. Can you give me another half hour?"

"I've given you half the night so I think I can manage another half hour."

"I'm really sorry. I am." Natalie reached across the table for Marcia's hand.

"Stop," Marcia said, hearing the forcefulness in her own voice, and Natalie pulled back.

The incident with Natalie did something to Marcia's insides. She felt it the rest of the day and that night when she lay down to go to sleep. Sleep did not come. She kept imagining what had happened to Natalie. Various scenarios flashed across the screen of her mind. Grubby hands grabbing at her clothes and spreading her legs while she lay on the floor, drugged and unconscious. Hands riffling through her pocketbook, removing cash as raucous laughter rained down from above. The sour smell in that hallway, the shouting from other apartments, occasional screams floating through the dank air, ignored.

Marcia leapt up from bed. She knew she would not be able to sleep. She'd called in sick at her department store job after dropping Natalie off, feeling too exhausted and upset to go in to work. She'd have to make sure her job was still there today. Rochelle exhaled loudly and flipped onto her side, still asleep.

Why or why, Natalie? She asked that question over and over. Yes, she'd had a shock. Yes, her parents had kept something from her. Well, her father had made the decision, and the mother had acquiesced. The usual scenario. Marcia slipped from bed and went over to the window, where she could look down at the street. All was quiet. The streetlights were shutting off, and one car slid slowly along, probably looking for a parking spot on the correct side for alternate side of the street parking. Marcia had been lucky on her return home as a car had just been pulling out on the side of the street she needed.

Had Natalie been looking for escape? Physical escape from her parents, her upbringing, her life? Or mental and emotional escape, from her disappointment, her confinement, her sense of betrayal? Whatever it was, how could Natalie let herself fall into such a situation? Marcia banged her head against the glass. Never will that happen to me, she whispered to the street below. She was certain Natalie knew more about what had happened than she was letting on. Do I really want to know more, Marcia asked herself. Natalie had seen Marcia's disgust and horror; Marcia was certain it had been written on her face. She couldn't hide it.

Hadn't Natalie been afraid? Maybe she, Marcia, was too much of a coward to go to some apartment with some guy she'd met on the street. She imagined him as dirty and grungy, with an unruly beard and rotten teeth and unwashed hair. Of course, dangerous people don't necessarily broadcast what they are in their looks, she knew, but she was convinced that if he had appeared clean-cut and neat and well-groomed, Natalie would have bolted. And she herself had met Gus on the street, she had to admit, but that was different, she believed. He was a Brooklyn College student, after all. Either way, Marcia was certain she would not have gone. But it wasn't cowardice, she insisted to herself. It was common sense, self-preservation. Would she ever feel so desperate, so lost and unhinged, that she would do what Natalie had done? Take a crazy chance like that? Let's hope not, she decided, turning back from the window.

And her poor dad. He'd always been angry and difficult, and now there was an explanation for that. What horrible things had those Nazis done to his wife's dead body, while he had to stand there helplessly? It was unimaginable. And now his pain has been transferred to Natalie, to live on in a different form. Does it go on forever?

CHAPTER FIFTEEN

"Marsh! Are you alone or is anyone else home?" Eliot's voice on the phone sounded different, like he was running – huffing and puffing – while talking.

"No one else is here."

"Good. I wanted to catch you alone. I have some amazing news. I want to tell you first."

"Sock it to me."

"I'm getting married."

"WHAT?!!!!"

Eliot was laughing. "Hey, I know it's sudden. I've been seeing this gal, Joanne. She's also from New York – and Jewish, by the way. She's been out here for a while, staying with a cousin. From the minute we met, we hit it off, and finally we decided to get engaged."

"This is a joke, right?"

"No joke, sis. And there's more." Eliot laughed again, and his laugh sounded unhinged. "She's got a six-year-old daughter, Elise, from a bad first marriage. Elise is the most terrific kid -- everyone will love her. She already calls me 'Daddy.'" He chuckled. "I plan to adopt her."

Marcia felt the wind knocked out of her, and she leaned against the wall, squinting into the kitchen, making sure everything was the same. Yup – the Formica table, the worn chairs, the shiny stove top with the chrome teakettle sitting primly atop it – all the same. Had Eliot lost his mind? Had her kind-hearted big brother been bewitched? Had this seductress used her cute little kid to entrap him? Would her brother, her ally, now be lost to her?

Don't pre-judge, Marcia chided herself, her head spinning. Eliot was always so reasonable. Maybe they are both really great and Eliot will be happy. It is his decision and his life. If I want to be respected for my decisions, I have to give my own brother the same.

"Marcia?"

"I'm here. I haven't fainted from shock yet. I guess you found a way to upstage me, huh?"

Another laugh. "Keep it to yourself for a while, all right?"

"Sure. But how do you plan to break this little tidbit of news?"

"We're coming back in a few weeks. We'll announce it then."

"What about grad school?"

"I plan to defer it for a year. I'll get a job in New York – got a few leads already – and then go at night." His words were gushing forth, a river flowing in excitement.

Marcia let out a huge sigh and slumped against the wall. One by one, we all take off, she thought, on our own time-tables and in our own ways. "I don't know what to say."

"Say congratulations and you are happy for me."

Her father knocked on her door that evening. That was unusual, she realized.

"Marcia," he said, stepping in. "It's good you visited Grandma and Grandpa this week. I'm glad you did."

Marcia bristled. Don't ruin it, she thought, directing that thought mentally to her father.

"I have something important to tell you now. I want you to listen."

Oh no, Marcia thought. Maybe he too, like Natalie's father, had some secret past. She closed her book and stood up.

He looked around the room, appearing somewhat uncomfortable. "Now don't start answering me back. Just listen. OK?"

She nodded.

"Every time you go into your apartment," he began, "lock the door behind you *immediately*. Do you hear me? Don't go put down your bag or groceries first. Turn around and lock the door first. Do you understand?" He was staring straight at her, his eyes small and beady, his mouth set in a tight line.

As she began to respond, he held up his hand. "At night, before you go to sleep, check that the door and windows are locked. And that the gas on the stove is off."

Marcia suddenly realized that she was now slightly taller than her dad. As she stared down at the top of his bald head, she felt so sorry for him. Of course, a snarky response was ready to spring from her lips at first, but in that moment of face to face, or face to head, encounter, she was filled with gratitude – and pity. She choked up.

"You don't have to worry, Dad. I will do all that," she answered in a gentle cadence. At least she hoped it was gentle to his ears.

"Good," he said. He nodded. "Good," he said again before turning to leave the room.

CHAPTER SIXTEEN

"Telephone for you," Marcia's mother announced, pointing the receiver toward her. "A... Professor Myers?"

"Oh!" Marcia bounded toward the phone, practically grabbing it from her mother's hand. Her favorite history professor was calling her at home!

"I hope this is not an inconvenient time," the professor said.

"No, of course not!"

"I just like to check in with my top students after they graduate. And you were certainly one of the top."

"Thank you." Marcia felt herself blushing.

"Do you know what you will be doing now?"

Marcia told her about the job she'd landed, and the professor was effusive in her enthusiasm. She knew the person who had been the chair of the department until four or five years ago, when he retired, and she had high praise for the quality of the education there. "Do you know what courses you will be teaching?" she asked.

"I will have two European history classes." The professor practically shrieked like a young girl. "How perfect!" European history was her forte and the course she taught at Brooklyn College. "You will be wonderful at that! Your feel for European history is so mature. I will always remember the paper you did on the Holocaust. It was brilliant. If you need any materials, please contact me."

"Thank you. I would love that," Marcia said, overcome.

"You know, I am not Jewish but my husband is," Professor Myers said. "I showed him your paper – did I mention that? Anyway, he had tears in his eyes at some of the sections."

"I…didn't know that. I appreciate your telling me."

"His parents emigrated from Hungary. Budapest. They went through a lot. They don't want to talk about it."

"That's very common."

"You're right. But it seems a shame not to know the facts, the history, to pass that on. But you can't force people to open up if they just can't do it."

"That's true." Marcia felt she was talking to a peer, not a professor.

"Stay in touch, dear. You have a fine career ahead of you."

Marcia hung up and remained standing near the phone. Bubbling in her chest was a fragrant stew of purpose, of pride, of sheer happiness. The blackness of the telephone made everything clear. One route led to all that Professor Myers represented. Another road led to a dark alleyway, chasing Natalie. And that alleyway might beckon from time to time, offering respite, release, escape. But she could be resolute. She could aim to be like Professor Myers.

Once she was ensconced in her own place, Marcia just knew, everything would fall into place. No more nightmares, no more tension and arguments. Just freedom, solitude, and her beckoning future.

Marcia patted the shiny receiver and turned to her room. She would begin packing some clothing and books to bring over to the apartment. With a song in her heart, she pulled a suitcase down from the closet shelf.

Made in the USA
Middletown, DE
27 July 2023

35810624R00061